D0948279

# Joe's World

*Books by Muriel Dobbin*

JOE'S WORLD 1983
TASTE FOR POWER 1980

# Joe's World

**by Muriel Dobbin**

Drawings by Muriel Dobbin and Jean Rather

**Atheneum New York 1983**

LIBRARY OF CONGRESS CATALOGING IN PUBLICATION DATA

*Dobbin, Muriel.*
*Joe's world.*

*1. Dogs—Fiction. I. Title.*
*PS3554.O145J6 1983 813'.54 83-45060*
*ISBN 0-689-11426-5*


*Published simultaneously in Canada by McClelland and Stewart Ltd.*
*Composed by Maryland Linotype Composition Company, Baltimore, Maryland*
*Manufactured by Fairfield Graphics, Fairfield, Pennsylvania*
*Designed by Mary Cregan*
*First Edition*

*For the real Joe, and the Jacobs, who raised him to be an inspiration*

*And for Ted, Jean, and, most of all, Elaine, without whom Joe would never have written anything*

# Joe's World

# Chapter 1

It isn't that I don't like him, but I've had to get rid of them before. They always seem to feel it's their duty to rescue her from her lifestyle, and since a lot of her life is centered around me, that is worrying. First they think She drinks too much and then they cause trouble because I like a martini or two at the end of the day myself. Or in the middle of it, depending on whether it's raining. How can you let that dog drink? they ask her, and She is a little embarrassed about the fact that She and I have been drinking together pretty much since I was a pup. She was a cub reporter then, and not flying around on big assignments the way She is now.

She used to defend me. He doesn't drink much, She would say. But since Charlie more or less moved in, it's been different. Charlie and I got along pretty well for a bit. He didn't disapprove of my drinking. But he made fun of it, which to my mind was worse. I used to think he invited people over just to watch me lap up a little gin, and they would all sit around shrieking with laughter. She knew I was embarrassed. I have always prided myself on my dignity, so She must have known I was embarrassed, even if I was the star of their parties. Half of them laughed themselves sick, and the rest just threatened to call the S.P.C.A. They were generally the ones who sniffed and said dogs don't drink.

Well, generally speaking, dogs don't drink, but most dogs don't have my problems. I mean, I have to look out for someone who, in my opinion, really can't take proper care of herself.

Many's the night She's cried until my fur was so wet I thought I'd get pneumonia, or at least rheumatism. And when She isn't home, which is a lot of the time, I get lonesome enough to have a small drink by myself in the shank of the evening, as they say. I seem to spend a lot of time watching her pack to fly off somewhere in one of those campaign planes She laughs about with her friends when She's at home. It was one of those times She was away that I began playing with her typewriter. I used to watch her pounding away at it, and it didn't look too difficult, especially once I figured out you had to push a button to start it. So I practiced a bit and it passed the time. Then I began putting things down. I mean, when I read some of the stuff She writes, not to mention some of her friends, the kind of thing I run into makes a lot more sense, at least in my world, which I consider a much more peaceful place than hers, because it deals with problems that are simple but not silly.

I must admit I do like the times when She's at home. I like listening to her and I think She likes talking to me. I like the sound of her voice, although I wish She wouldn't talk baby talk to me. She has a soft voice and She doesn't often shout, and She hardly ever cries because She knows it troubles me. There was a time one of the men She brought home made her cry and I bit him. It seemed like the thing to do at the time, and the way She hugged me after he went slamming out, I knew She was pretty pleased about it. We finished off the martinis together that night.

I think that's what disturbs me about this thing with Charlie. I haven't had any trouble getting rid of the others, and She's always seemed glad of it. But with Charlie, it's been different. She met Charlie just after She broke up with Tim, and I have to admit, by comparison, Charlie was an immense improvement. Tim was thirty-four going on fourteen, and a member of that breed who say they love a woman who is liberated, then sulk when she doesn't do the laundry. He kept explaining to her how sensitive he was, and he criticized her all the time for not realizing how She was denting his sensitivities. By the time I decided the moment was right to dent something else, She was a walking mass of guilt. And as he left, he accused her of putting me up to biting him in what I have to say was a sensitive spot. She cried into her martinis until the vermouth turned to salt, and I was actually grateful when a week later She came home and said She had met somebody who was a lawyer and who took care of her.

I should have been warned by that phrase, because She'd always relied on me to take care of her. But Charlie was nice to her. He didn't want her to take care of him, that was true, although it seemed to be mostly because he didn't think anybody could do anything better than he could. But he made a great fuss over her, and he had the sense to make a great fuss over me. That was before he discovered we drank together, and then he started braying like a donkey about my capacity for gin. When She laughed, just a little, along with him, I knew I was in for trouble. And I didn't have any excuse to bite him; I consider violence a tactic of last resort.

Charlie obviously is going to require a more subtle strategy, and I try not to think about what will happen if that doesn't work. She talks about him as if he's always going to be with us, and won't that be nice? I deliberately do not wag my tail, but She's so besotted about him, I don't know if She notices as much as She usually does. I'm cool toward him, of course, but he is so all over her that She doesn't notice that either. Once or twice he's tried to close the door in my face, but I took care of that. I sulked so much when he suggested that maybe I should go to obedience school—at my age?—they almost had their first fight. Unfortunately, he's a fast learner, and he never picked on me again.

I think the worst thing is that he occupies so much of her time. She doesn't have much time left over from her job, anyway, so I practically don't see her any more. She's out with him right now, and even if She does come home, which She doesn't always, he'll probably be with her, which means She and I can't be cozy the way we used to. It's funny how much it annoys me that he laughs at my drinking, because She used to sort of giggle, but that was different. And She might not have giggled either if she'd known how much I drank, because it costs her a lot more than Bonzo's Munch Bones.

We've been together a long time and, as you can probably tell, I'm very fond of her, although I can't understand why anyone would get paid for wandering around writing down the silly things other people say.

But, She does get paid, and we live in a nice house with plenty to eat for both of us and almost enough gin. It's sort of a town house, I think they call it, and it has a nice backyard with a big shady tree and roses that climb up the fence so I can sniff them when I'm napping on a hot afternoon. There are other town houses in this complex, which has a swimming pool and a lot of grass and places to wander. And a lot of the other residents also are sensible enough to have animals, even if some of them are cats.

For example, there is my cousin Joseph, who lives three doors away, and is older than me. His mission in life, apart from sleeping, is giving advice to other golden retrievers. He says other dogs don't count because they don't have our distinguished ancestry. I'm not averse to compliments on my lineage, of course, but I must say I've encountered a number of remarkably dense dogs of my own breed. Like Gracie, who had trouble telling up from down when it came to stairs and who once got banned from a friend's home because she helped him eat the sofa. Or Dickens, who swallowed several brass padlocks, more or less because he couldn't think of anything else to do with them. Or Tyler, whose passion for pursuing cars almost caused him to need a tail implant.

And of course when you get to other breeds, it gets worse. I mean, there's Alfred P. Quagmire, an exotic but energetic white creature, who looks like he was knitted. No golden retriever I know would have taken on a bottle of glue, although a pup I know called Gusty did try to eat his own bed until he found it was filled with woodchips. And a friend called Taffy conducts an unending war with flower pots, which she considers a version of the MX.

Anyway, at least in my world we can tell a golden retriever from a cocker spaniel, which is more than I can say for the magazine editors who printed a photograph of Vice President Bush and his wife with their golden retriever C. Fred Bush. C. Fred, as far as I could tell, was unquestionably a cocker spaniel, and nobody ever suggested that by night all dogs were gray. But that does lead me to my grievance that in the literary world, at least, dogs seem to be taking a second place to cats.

I believe dogs have been done an injustice in terms of public recognition, which was another reason I began this journal. For example, I find reading the bestseller list of the *New York Times* book review section downright discouraging. What is this national passion with cats? The only memorable thing I know about cats is that the ancient Egyptians used to shave off their eyebrows when their cat died. But I seriously doubt that was the kind of animal who would do a sort of frozen samba on television, which is the kind of thing animals stoop to nowadays to keep their owners in cash.

I know a couple of cats in my neighborhood who seem pretty normal. Like Terminal Hate down the block; there's a cat who despises the world, and just about anybody would respect him. Rhinestone Cowcat is a pretty tough little cookie, too, in spite of that silly collar her owner puts around her neck. But Joseph and I have been wondering whatever happened to dogs? I mean, you can still see those old Rin Tin Tin and Lassie movies on late-night television. Those were dogs in the true tradition of man's best friend. Not that I have anything against Benjie or Old Yeller or Big Red, but I had a severe case of the heaves over that mechanical animal, Chomps, that Hollywood came up with. You would think there were enough good dogs out of work without their concocting something made of foam rubber and imported fur.

She's told me about political dogs She has known,

and I wouldn't care for that kind of a dog's life. Roosevelt's Fala, from what I have read, seemed like a decent, down-to-earth Scottie, and Bobby Kennedy's Brumas and Freckles were fairly normal animals who got away with disgracing themselves in fancy restaurants. But those beagles who belonged to LBJ, they had my sympathy. In addition to being saddled with those idiotic names—what self-respecting dog could go through life answering to "Here, Her! Here, Him!" —they had to submit to being picked up by their ears. Anyone who picked me up by the ears would get molars in his wrist, Secret Service or no Secret Service. Then there was Johnson's collie, Blanco, the one She told me was so nervous it had to be given tranquilizers, or "gentlers," as its owner called them. It was probably a good deal too gentle to be taken on walks with fifty flat-footed reporters tripping on its back paws. Very unnerving!

But this cat fad is typical of the kind of thing people do. They have so little perception of what lies beyond the narrow boundaries of their own noses. For example, She says She knows I understand every word She says, and sometimes She thinks I'm about to talk back to her. But as I said to Joseph, why should I talk back to her? What would I say that She would understand? Would any of them understand my world, where there are no hours or schedules or trains and planes and buses, where there are only the passing of time, and the birds and bugs and mice, and even cats.

This is the world that has always been, a world where there is always time to do something really important, like stop and talk to a melancholy mouse or watch the sunlight fall on the foliage of an oak tree, or smell the fragrance of roses in wet grass. The only time people care about sunlight is when they're out by their pools, turning themselves peculiar and violent shades of red. They never seem to take time to sit and watch quietly, and I think that's because they're afraid to be alone. They carry their noise with them in those ugly boxes that make it impossible to hear rain on the roof. And the sad part is, you can learn a lot just lying in the grass waiting for an interesting bug to come along. Children know that, but adults are too stupid to remember it, which is why so many children grow up seeing nothing but the television screen, which is the equivalent of growing up inside a kaleidoscope full of violent color and movement, meaning nothing.

She likes to watch old movies on television, which was how I came to know about the dog films. And we've had a few good laughs over animal commercials. She says that whenever I see a dog in one of those ridiculous advertisements, I whiffle, which I suppose is a good enough term for what I consider a dignified, if gruff, chuckle. Cats don't think those commercials are funny, but they know there's money in them. Perhaps one of the reasons cats are so popular these days is that they are in tune with the selfishness of the age.

Most cats I know are pragmatists and proud of it. Dogs are the only idealists left in the world, and if you don't believe me, just think of the way a dog owner is greeted when he comes home and then compare that scene to the homecoming of a cat owner. The dog owner walks through the door and the dog is bounding up, tail wagging, eyes shining, ears perked, just vibrating with eagerness to bring slippers, carry the paper, lick a hand, fix a drink.

The cat owner walks in and the cat raises its head languidly from the best armchair and says, you're late, where's my dinner, am I expected to wait around and starve while you're out slopping it up in some disgusting bar? Intimidated, the cat owner rushes to the kitchen without taking his coat off, opens a can, mixes things up, freshens the water in the cat dish, all the while making nauseating mewing sounds to ingratiate himself with His Majesty, who is still curled up in the living room and may or may not emit a perfunctory purr in response to all this attention.

The devoted dog-next-door will, of course, wait patiently for his dinner while the owner has a drink or two, reads the paper, and considers his own menu for the evening. Some dogs forget their manners and get rude when their stomachs have rumbled enough. But a well-trained dog owner requires only the merest nudge of a reminder. Just enough to knock the newspaper out of his hand will do it, I have found.

Nobody seems to realize that when you look into a cat's eyes, what you're seeing is usually pure contempt. I watch people fawning over Terminal Hate, and I know he's barely restraining himself from laying their wristbones bare. He's done that once or twice, but of course he was forgiven. Dogs bite only for good reason; they're remarkably patient about having their ears rubbed the wrong way or having to sit and listen to nonsense. A cat's expression tends to discourage nonsense.

Even Joseph was complaining the other day about the amount of time his owners spend worrying about their electricity bills. He kept wondering why they didn't just build a fire or put on a sweater and think about something more useful. That's significant, because Joseph isn't always too alert. He has never left our world, and he says a lot of my restlessness is a result of the fact that I keep putting at least one paw over the doorstep into the world of people, which would depress any dog. I found this a remarkably astute statement coming from Joseph because, although he is a relative and I am fond of him, I have to suspect that if you picked up one of his ear flaps, you might see clear through to the other side of his head.

Joseph is not exactly retarded, but I think that affair his mother had with an over-the-hill boxer diminished his natural intelligence. As he said rather cynically once, his mother was known in the neighborhood as Terminal Heat. And Joseph is the only dog I know who can't remember why he's standing beside a tree with one leg raised.

Perhaps Joseph's charm lies in his capacity for self-containment and contentment. I have rarely known him to be ruffled, even when poked by small children. He avoids looking at newspapers and the only thing I have ever seen him read is Henry James, which he said he found edifying without being disruptive to the soul. For myself, I prefer Thurber. There was a man who understood dogs. There was nothing cute about Thurber's animals; he treated them like adults and that's how they acted. I think a lot of decent dogs have been corrupted nowadays. The worst of them have begun to act like people and that's a sad state of affairs for a dog. I believe it was Thurber who said man was trying to drag dogs down to his level, and he may have been right.

Joseph says I spend too much time worrying about people, but the thing is, I feel sorry for them because they miss so much. They move so fast they rarely see anything, and if they do, unless it has a designer label on it, they don't want it. They don't seem to realize that a lot of things haven't changed for a very long time and, well . . . take buttercups; they are just what they seem to be, no better and no worse, and that's probably how it's supposed to be. Not even kings or presidents or politicians have managed to change that. Mine is a world where buttercups are important, and one of the reasons I am fond of her is that I think She has a glimmering of that.

In a sense, I consider her a subject for research. Her world doesn't make much sense to me, and mine is probably as much of a mystery to her. I suppose that's why I finally decided to make use of my new typing skill and put down, for whomever may one day read it, this glimpse of a world where people have no place, not only because they have lost sight of that world but, sadly, because they have lost their place in it. It is certainly a world without politicians, whom I do not consider people. She was writing a long story the other day analyzing the election chances of a presidential candidate who seems to me to be on the intellectual level of Rhinestone Cowcat, a dingbat of a cat if ever there was one. To be candid, I have lost the ability to tell one politician from another. I can understand that they all want the same thing. What I can't understand is why they all sound alike. Most political speeches should be chopped up and sold as sedatives.

Joseph listened to a lengthy political speech once, and slept so long afterward, his owners called the vet. But I understood his reaction. Although I have more curiosity about people than Joseph, I find myself nodding off whenever somebody stands up and declares himself dedicated to doing good for mankind instead of coming right out and admitting he can't wait to get his paws on all those perks that go with holding office, and that he's just drooling for the junkets and joyrides—not to mention the groupies—and don't let anyone tell me he would faint dead away at the thought of a little comfy corruption to pad his bank account.

Politics is entertaining, of course, and not quite as violent as the movies, but nobody ever seems to admit he's running because he's desperate to boss people around and never mind all this malarkey about saving his fellow citizens. Most of them have a lot in common with those religious fellows, who seem to feel they've cornered the market on salvation.

My paw is getting tired, so I think I'll stop and put my journal away under the refrigerator, which is convenient to the gin, and anyway She never cleans under there. Which reminds me, She's running low on gin, and I expect She and Charlie will finish what's left of it if they do come home. It's getting late, so maybe She'll stay over at his place again, which I suppose means I can finish the gin myself, but on the other hand, I don't want him snickering at me again when they find the empty bottle. And of course it would be a good deal more embarrassing to have them find me typing. If he thinks it's funny that a dog drinks, he might laugh himself into a heart attack over a dog keeping a journal. Which may be something I should keep in mind, the way things are going.

# Chapter 2

Well, it was just as well I got things tidied up, with my journal under the refrigerator and the typewriter turned off, because they came home a few minutes later. Not that they would have noticed if I had been writing with a quill pen and a copy of Bartlett's beside me, because I could tell that they had far exceeded my modest intake of martinis. She came and put her arms around my neck and said She was sorry my dinner was late, and Charlie said ho-ho, he supposed ol' Joe there had been having a few pre-dinner drinks anyway, how about that, Joe ol' boy, ol' boy? I ignored him, and hoped She'd notice the difference between his behavior when imbibing, and mine. I might have bumped into the kitchen door once or twice, but I am confident I've never been undignified. When they finally showed signs of staggering off to bed, I decided to sleep in the backyard. It was a warm evening, and I had the distinct impression that my presence would not be missed.

Which meant I was up earlier than usual, and since they were still in bed I had some breakfast and decided to go for a walk and visit my friends. It proved to be interesting, but not entirely restful, mostly because of Terminal Hate's bad temper, which is something I'm pretty well used to—nobody living within a half-mile radius of him could be unaware of his rages—but now and again feline illogicality wearies me.

Yet, Terminal Hate and I usually get along pretty well because, as far as cats are concerned, I believe in live and let live and, in any case, I don't know that I could beat him in an all-out fight; he has a mean left claw, and he's not above fighting dirty. Today, however, he was in a rage because he had heard about a new proposal by the animal control and welfare commission to make cat owners pay a registration fee for their felines and, not only that, to require cats to wear collars. When I pointed out that a lot of cats already wore collars for identification and it seemed like a pretty sensible idea, T.H. spat at me.

Only *dogs* wore collars, he said; no cat worthy of its mice would be caught dead in a stupid collar. I said, with some restraint, I thought, that wearing a collar, especially one of the normal leather variety—not that monstrosity Rhinestone Cowcat has buckled around her neck—might prevent one from ending one's days as a victim of the local gas chamber. Terminal Hate said he had a relative who had ended up hanging from a tree when his goddamned cute red-leather collar got caught on a branch just as he was making a really spectacular pounce on a thrush.

Cats, said Terminal Hate in a hoarse hiss, were constitutionally entitled to life, liberty, and the pursuit of anything they wanted to eat. I said that might be, but dogs had rights, too, and as far as collars went I thought he was being a trifle hysterical about the whole thing. He said I was the only dog he had ever met whose eyes he hadn't tried to claw out and he was beginning to think he had made an error in judgment.

My cousin Joseph came by at that point, which didn't really help, because Terminal Hate despises Joseph. He has never learned to respect Joseph's good qualities, one of which is what I have sometimes thought of as an astounding inability to tell a dog from a cat. It gives Joseph an attitude of goodwill toward all, but it can be confusing to a lot of cats, and it seems to infuriate Terminal Hate, who is something of a basic thinker. He believes in upholding simple standards and not cluttering his mind with compromises.

Joseph said he thought collars were rather nice. He had always worn a collar and it had never troubled him except when he absent-mindedly ate part of it during dinner one night. By this time Terminal Hate's eyes had become pure yellow slits, which I have come to recognize as a sign of approaching fury. So I suggested to Joseph, as tactfully as I could, that we should be on our way. Terminal Hate said rather nastily at that point that I might as well get along while I could still walk. I could hardly ignore that kind of unpleasantness, so I asked very coolly what he meant.

His owners, he said, stropping his claws, had mentioned in his hearing the other night that I seemed to be overdoing it a bit. The bottle, he added, when I stared at him. I said I had no idea what they were talking about and it said very little for his owners' idea of intelligent conversation to indulge in that kind of gossip. Terminal Hate said he thought his owners were weak-minded fools, but he could see what he could see, and he had seen me staggering home more than once, and wasn't that what humans called a potbellery I was developing. I said the word was potbelly and I certainly had no such thing although I might have a touch of thickening around the middle, which was the consequence, I admitted, of too little exercise. Terminal Hate sneered.

Had I heard, he asked, of that canine alcoholic over on Tenth Street? The one who had been pub crawling? I said I might have encountered him from time to time and he had seemed like an extraordinarily jovial and well-mannered Labrador with a nice line in witticisms, which was more than I could say of present company. Terminal Hate said the Labrador had been taken to the vet recently and turned out to have a beer belly and cirrhosis of the liver, not to mention being thirty pounds overweight. Moreover, he went on, still stropping those ugly claws of his, the Lab's owner had told the doctor that he couldn't keep up with Tommy's drinking bouts. Personally, he never touched anything but milk, said Terminal Hate, and he just thought as a friend he should mention these things.

I was really exasperated, and I thought Joseph might have given me a little moral support. I mean, Joseph has been with me when I've had a drink or two, and he could have testified that I can handle my liquor. But Joseph, as usual, was asleep, quite literally on Terminal Hate's doorstep. T.H. had sneered himself almost into a good mood by that point, and he began washing his face—presumably in preparation for his evening's bloodletting. So he was taken by surprise when I said I understood he was going to audition for a television commercial, which, I assumed, was why he was paying such attention to his appearance.

What the hell was I talking about, he demanded. Pleased that I could at least ruffle his fur I said my owner had told me there was an audition to be held for especially evil and ugly cats. The winner would receive a "Bad Kitty of the Month" button. I said I understood his owners were sure that he would be a shoo-in and I could hardly wait to see him wearing his button. On his new collar, I added with temerity. Terminal Hate, who despises the mere word "kitty" and who once almost detached a small boy's ear for using it in his presence, bristled in a manner that made even Joseph stir in his sleep. He said I was making it up and they wouldn't dare. I'll claw their eyes out, he said, I don't mind being ugly but I'm no kitty. I was just trying to make trouble for him, he said, and he knew what to do with fat, drunk dogs who were troublemakers.

I said I had no time for brawling, bad-tempered cats and if he couldn't recognize some friendly advice when he heard it, then I was not to be held responsible. After all, I said patiently, hadn't I been appreciative of his kind words of warning about the scurrilous gossip regarding my occasional libations? I said I was surprised at him; I had always considered him the most intelligent member of his breed (not mentioning that I didn't consider that much of a compliment) and if this was how he was going to behave with an old friend and neighbor then I would have my little chats with Rhinestone Cowcat, who at least was always pleasant. Terminal Hate was taken aback; he never has been able to cope with reason or restraint and it clearly hurt his pride that he might be replaced by Cowcat, who admittedly is a butterfly brain, even for a cat.

He said gruffly that there was no offense meant and none taken but he had to be going about his business and there had better not be any damned audition or his owners would wonder what had hit them when they got home. I said quite stiffly that I wished him good day and nudged Joseph in the ribs. I wanted to get away before Terminal Hate decided I really had insulted him. Anything I can't talk my way out of nowadays I don't really want to get into.

Joseph, who had missed most of it as usual, blinked at Terminal Hate and said he hoped he would win the kitty award. I could see that choleric look returning to T.H.'s eyes, so we left rather quickly.

When I got home, they were already gone, so I decided to have a small martini, even though it was still morning. I began to meditate on what Terminal Hate had said about my drinking. I could not imagine that She was so disloyal as to talk about our private life, so I had to conclude that Charlie was babbling around the neighborhood about this Dog Who Drank. I was probably the laughingstock of local dinner parties. Lapping up the last of the gin, I decided I would have to become more alert to Charlie's weaknesses. I was in residence, after all, which gave me an advantage; I had known her a lot longer than he had, and would, I hoped, know her long after he had gone. The trouble was that for the first time I had to consider one of her friends a rival. They had passed through my life before, but I'd hardly noticed until one of them upset her. There never before had been any doubt that She would return to me.

I felt my fur stand on end at the thought that Charlie might be different, and pawed out the bottle at the back of the liquor cabinet where she keeps an emergency supply. I needed to think, and another martini seemed like an admirable way to clear my head. Or it did at the time.

# Chapter 3

She didn't get home until long after midnight and perhaps it was just as well because she didn't notice how much I had drunk. But She was up early this morning, rattling around and complaining about a hangover and having to go to a news conference about the threat to the nation that is supposedly posed, if you can believe it, by the Mediterranean fruit fly. I expect it was being awakened by the noise of the coffee pot that gave me such a headache. Of course I got up and was friendly and, after I drank a lot of water—She forgot to put ice cubes in it again—I felt a little better. At least Charlie wasn't there trying to make cheerful conversation during breakfast. I took a short nap after She left and when I woke up I noticed that the morning paper was filled with suggestions that the fruit fly was responsible for everything short of the sky falling. So, I thought I'd take a stroll over to the vegetable plot, which really isn't much of a plot because most people seem to plant things without being sure what they're going to turn into, and then they grumble when something unexpected pops up. People can be difficult with growing things, I have noticed.

What seems to upset them most is when, in the natural course of events, some of their pet plants are nibbled a little by bugs. Nobody seems to take into account that bugs have to eat, too. It has occurred to me that there should be some sort of middle ground between the people who want to spray every bug in the world to death and those who are willing to let the bugs eat everything in the world. Sometimes I consider myself fortunate to be merely an interested observer.

As it happened, the first person I ran into at the vegetable plot was a Med fly looking as bedraggled as you might expect of a hunted creature. At the best of times those insects have bloodshot eyes and droopy wings, not to mention sticky feet, which I understand are quite important to their operation, but this one looked as if it had walked through a hundred miles of mud. She said her name was Mame and that she had been on the road so long her feet were killing her and she was seriously thinking of heading for Mexico if her wings held out. I felt sorry for Mame, because as far as I can see, the Med fly's chief crime is what I must admit is an unusually voracious appetite for fruit; any kind of fruit. As I understand it, they are partial to two hundred different species, and I can see that the people who grow fruit for a living would have a problem finding customers if every pear and peach bore the mark of a fruit fly's teeth. It is understandable that they would want to discourage such gluttony, but I don't have much patience with the way they have been demolishing the poor things' sex life.

According to Mame, all the fellows she had met recently had flown in from Hawaii. Instead of being suntanned studs, however, they had been turned into a bunch of eunuchs by the sterilization program that's currently underway. Mame said some people would have called it genocide, but fruit flies have few champions.

The whole thing made her so angry, she went on, that she had single-handedly chewed up two orchards and a vegetable field. And as if things weren't bad enough now they had helicopters out dive-bombing her. I asked if she meant the aerial spraying that I had been reading about, and she said that was a pretty way of putting it. Malathion she admitted, brushing mud off her orange and yellow wings, was killing a lot of Med flies but, in a way, all this persecution might do some good if it made members of the insect world realize they had to stick together in order to survive. Fruit flies weren't nearly as indestructible as cockroaches, said Mame, although they were a lot prettier, but this martyrdom her species was enduring might teach the multi-leggeds a lesson about not eating each other.

I said it might make her feel better to know that an entomologist—Mame shuddered at the word—had reported that all these chemicals people had been showering on bugs had actually produced a reverse effect. She looked puzzled and said she didn't care for the use of the word "bug," but she would let it pass. I apologized and told her that according to this man the spraying was actually producing a superbug—begging her pardon. She asked did I mean a fly in a blue suit with a red S on it, and I suppressed a sigh and said, no, I meant the kind of fly that could thrive because of all the efforts made to kill it. I was beginning to be sorry I had mentioned it because Mame clearly was confused, and I didn't think her mind was too sharp to start with, or if it was, maybe the Malathion had dimmed it. But I tried to explain that some flies could now swallow a dose of DDT—Mame shuddered again—that once would have done in fifty thousand of its kind, and fly off happily.

She said I was making it up and looked even more bemused when I said it was a matter of genetic variations. However, she obviously had decided that whatever I was saying it was the only good news she had heard that week. Her wings had lost some of their droopiness and she looked as if she might indeed make it to Mexico. I was about to wish her well and be on my way—I was becoming a little bored, to tell the truth—when I heard a cough, and noticed a rather lonely looking bug with a thoughtful expression sitting on a potato leaf. He apparently had been listening to Mame's troubles. I asked if he had just flown into town, and he said, a touch pompously, I thought, that he was a Nantucket Pine Tip Moth and, if I was unfamiliar with the species, that was the moth that could steal Christmas.

Mame said she didn't think that was anything to boast about, and Pine Tip retorted that he was more selective in his diet than she was. To prevent the conversation from degenerating into a vulgar squabble, and because I suspected he might be a little envious of the Med flies' publicity, I asked how his species had acquired such a reputation. He explained that his people had hitchhiked from New England, where the flavor of the treetops was declining and the chemical spray was beginning to give them indigestion. Mame, who evidently liked to dominate the conversation, said there was nothing he could tell her about getting an upset stomach from chemical spray. Pine Tip ignored her and said the move to California had really been a matter of improving the quality of their nutrition, which seemed to me to be quite reasonable.

I still wasn't clear about Christmas, I said, and Pine Tip told me he thought the impact of their arrival had been exaggerated, although it was true that his species could take a good chunk out of a Monterey Pine, which were a prime kind of Christmas tree. Mame said viciously that she hoped they'd eat every tree in the country after what the Med flies had suffered for taking a few bites of fruit. I decided that while I had sympathy for Mame she was vastly underrating the fruit fly's capacity for greens. I said I had better be moving along. Mame, who seemed to be something of a gossip, asked if I had heard about the juniper miner moths and what they were likely to do to the gin business.

I paused at that and admitted I had heard nothing of juniper miner moths, and what did they have to do with gin? Mame said she understood the moths' impact on junipers could have some effect on the liquor market and anything that caused the two-leggeds trouble was fine with her. She had always felt, she said, that people who drank liquor deserved what they got. I said that everyone was entitled to his own taste in food and drink. She said she personally was opposed to stimulants of all kinds, which was why she hated that damned Malathion, and gin was just as bad.

It was clear I had misjudged her personality. I cocked my head and said callously that I thought I heard a helicopter, which made her check her feet and wings and take off. The Nantucket Pine Tip twitched his wings understandingly at me and said he had enjoyed a little eggnog in his day.

I was on my way home, noticing that my headache

had come back and contemplating the possibility that there might be some Bloody Mary mix left. I supposed Charlie would find it even funnier to see a dog with a hangover, and I hoped he had not decided to take the afternoon off and come over to fix her a surprise dinner, as he occasionally did. He could work on a brief at her place as easily as in his office, he told her, and She was touched by his thoughtfulness. I noticed that. Something had to explain her throwing her arms around his neck instead of mine when She came home. I wasn't really looking where I was going, I was so preoccupied about Charlie, and it gave my head an awful jolt when I heard this high-pitched squeaking sound between my front feet. I looked down to see the maddest worm I ever encountered.

More than a little weary of querulous insects at this point, I didn't quite feel up to dealing with an enraged worm, but I felt I owed him a little common courtesy, so I asked what was the matter. Other than my almost squashing him with my great hoof? he asked. I decided not to argue the semantic point. Well, if I really wanted to know, he continued, he had been listening to that fruit fly with dirty feet complaining and, in his opinion, she had no grounds for grumbling. At least, fruit flies had wings to fly with, he said, whereas worms were in a perpetual state of peril. And, to make matters worse, he had just heard that the state farm bureau was setting up a vermiculture department to help those monsters who ran worm farms. That was really the last straw.

I said I had never heard of a worm farm, and the worm said that was the trouble, worms were ignored by the national media, even though they were being sold like dirt to would-be farmers who just wanted them to reproduce like a hutchful of rabbits. I said I was sorry, but until I met him I had thought the chief problem for the worm was to avoid becoming bait. The worm's tail thrashed, and he said I was obviously unaware that his breed was so rich in protein it could be turned into delicious spaghetti, even if the thought did make him quiver all over. The thought made me quiver all over, too, and I could feel my stomach churning as I asked—worm spaghetti?

He assured me that it was considered a delicacy, and at that point I decided I really had to get home, so I stepped over him and left, before he could give me the recipe.

# Chapter 4

I was pleased to find that nobody was home when I got there, especially no Charlie. But he had mixed up some Bloody Marys and obviously left enough for later, so I took malicious pleasure in drinking the whole batch. It also soothed my nerves and my stomach, which were still jangling jointly from the thought of worm spaghetti. Charles would be annoyed when he got home, but he would hardly be able to blame me without upsetting her, because I knew She would defend me against any accusation that I drank Bloody Marys as well as martinis. She cherishes the illusion that I only drink a splash to keep her company, although it seems to me that Bloody Marys are a fairly obvious corollary to gin. I was feeling a little better by then, and decided that perhaps guerrilla warfare would be the best approach to my problem. Biting him at this stage clearly would be counter-productive. She might just marry him out of sympathy. What I had to do was make him look silly, because She has a fine sense of the ridiculous, and would be unlikely to want to live with somebody she laughed at.

*Chapter 4*

I felt so relieved after making my decision that I got out my journal and typed up my recollections of the morning, although the sound of the keys striking the paper was quite painful. After that, I felt I owed it to myself to lie down in the backyard beneath my favorite oak tree and gather my strength. I had hardly closed my eyes, however, when I heard a scratching sound, and I peeped upward cautiously to see Rhinestone Cowcat sitting on the wall above me, looking pensive.

I was beginning to think there was some kind of conspiracy to keep me from getting my rest, but I am fond of Rhinestone Cowcat who has a somewhat wistful quality, perhaps because Terminal Hate is always bullying her. He doesn't beat her up, which is better than the way he treats other cats, but he does order her around, which may be why she always seems to be looking over her shoulder, although it could be just an irritation from that silly collar her owner makes her wear. Anyway, I didn't feel I could ignore her. I knew she wouldn't come down, so I got up in order to look at her without getting a crick in my neck. We have been friends for years, but she still has an old-fashioned uneasiness about dogs. Rhinestone Cowcat is not very liberated, I am afraid, and her relationship with Terminal Hate reflects that aspect of her personality. She seems to feel that to be charming, she must be vague, or act as if she is. I usually find her entertaining, although not always when I am hung over.

She said she hoped she wasn't disturbing me, and asked if I had been asleep, which is the kind of question she is inclined to ask; purring the obvious, as Terminal Hate puts it. I sighed and said, no, and hoped she wasn't planning to stay long. But she looked so pleased to see me that I decided to tell her about Mame and the Nantucket moth and the worm. Rhinestone Cowcat shuddered and said I always met such interesting people. She washed her face in a manner that signified she had something on her mind, and said she, too, had had a couple of strange encounters recently. I asked what she meant and she said, well, mice. I waited, there being no way to speed up Rhinestone Cowcat when she is bestowing information, and she asked rather hesitantly if I had run into Wilbur.

I said, no, offhand I could recall no Wilburs among the mice of my acquaintance, and she said if I had met him, she was sure I would remember him because he was bald. All-over bald? I asked, and she said, yes, her whiskers quivering hysterically, I thought. I considered. Perhaps Wilbur had been in an accident, I suggested. Rhinestone Cowcat shook her head. She had been so upset by his appearance, she said, that she had forgotten all her mother had told her about the Instant Pounce technique and had stood there staring, until he asked her where her manners were.

After that, she said, she could hardly leap on him, at least not while they were engaged in civilized conversation and, in any case, she didn't think she would feel quite right about chewing on a bald mouse. I asked if she had found out why he was bald and she said that was the spooky part. He had explained that he was born hairless because he was part of an experiment. Ah, I said, he was a laboratory mouse.

Rhinestone Cowcat looked at me reproachfully. He was a very sad mouse, she said, because he had very few friends. Other mice tended to laugh at him, and also he was cold all the time. Why had he left the laboratory, I asked. Rhinestone Cowcat wanted to know whether I would stay in a laboratory if they left my cage door open, and I said it would depend on what they were doing to me in the laboratory. She said they weren't actually doing anything to Wilbur, he was a member of a very special breed of mouse that was being used for cancer research.

Wilbur had cancer? I asked. She said rather indignantly that she didn't know, but she did not think it was natural for a mouse to be running around naked, so to speak, and she thought I might be more sympathetic to a poor runaway. I pointed out that if Terminal Hate ran across Wilbur, his holiday from the laboratory, if that's what it was, would certainly come to an immediate and unhappy conclusion. Terminal Hate was unlikely to have any compunction about eating a hairless mouse. Rhinestone Cowcat said she had expected some refinement from me. She had thought I might help Wilbur avoid being hunted down.

I said I would be glad to protect any persecuted creature, but I was still unclear as to what she wanted me to do. Rhinestone Cowcat folded her paws under her primly and said that if I would just be quiet for a moment she would be happy to tell me. This kind of remark drives us all crazy, but as Terminal Hate points out, there isn't very much you can do except swat her one, and I try to restrain those impulses where some cats are concerned because I consider them inferior intellectually and therefore to be humored; rather like certain people.

Rhinestone Cowcat said Wilbur had told her he was a very special creature, a mutant mouse who was vulnerable to bacteria in the outside world. Which was why he had been living in her owner's medicine cabinet. I said I didn't think that was all that hygienic and Rhinestone Cowcat said to put it mildly it wasn't; you could practically grow penicillin in most of her owner's closets and the medicine cabinet was no exception. So where was Wilbur now? I asked. Rhinestone Cowcat said that was what she had been trying to tell me, except I had kept interrupting her. He was in my owner's refrigerator. That made me momentarily forget my headache. Why? I asked. Rhinestone Cowcat said she thought he would be safe from infection there. I said he probably would freeze to death, since he was bald, and she shook her head, no, he wouldn't because Christopher had placed him in a state of suspended animation.

I put my head back down on my paws; I was beginning to feel dizzy, an effect that Rhinestone Cowcat often has on me. I was beginning to understand why my cousin Joseph simply went to sleep, or pretended he did, every time he saw her. I wanted desperately to forget the whole thing, but I could imagine how She would react to finding Wilbur in the refrigerator. So I asked with as much patience as I could muster who Christopher was.

Rhinestone Cowcat said Christopher was a mouse. I nodded and waited. He was also a fugitive from a laboratory, she said, and I couldn't help wondering why all these mice were flooding out of laboratories all at once and invading my neighborhood. Why didn't the scientists take better care of their charges? Was Christopher bald, too? I asked. No, she said, Christopher had been taking part in a hibernation experiment. They were trying to find out whether you lived longer if you achieved suspended animation. Did you? I asked. That was what Christopher was trying to find out, said Rhinestone Cowcat, but he had gotten bored with sleeping in the cold and that was why he had left; he wanted a little sun. But it did look as if the experiment worked, because his parents, who had been trained to live in cold temperatures and sleep a lot, had lived four times as long as your average mouse.

It occurred to me that the solution to my own problems might be to climb into the refrigerator and take a nap, but Rhinestone Cowcat was looking at me impatiently, apparently waiting for me to solve the whole thing for her, as usual.

I said I was sorry to be so dense, but how did it help a bald mouse to sit inside a refrigerator? She said, well, of course, Christopher had taught Wilbur how to hibernate, and at that temperature he would be safe from germs. I watched Rhinestone Cowcat daintily scratching at a flea that had settled in near her collar. Suddenly she jumped up in exasperation, twitched her tail, and said the only reason she had stopped was to ask me to be kind to Wilbur and Christopher and to be sure She didn't murder them when She opened the refrigerator.

I lay down and thought for a while after Rhinestone Cowcat had gone, wondering what to do about Wilbur and Christopher. I supposed I could carry them off somewhere safe, but if Rhinestone Cowcat was right, and there was, of course, no reason to suppose she was, they might not be able to survive outside the refrigerator. They were, however, equally unlikely to survive when She opened the refrigerator section they were in. I wasn't sure whether they had to be frozen or just cold. For all I knew, they might be mice Popsicles by now. I thought wistfully that it might be nice if Charlie were the one to find Wilbur and Christopher. His reaction might be disgust at the thought that She was such a poor housekeeper that there were mice in her refrigerator. I decided I was indulging in pipe dreams, because Charlie would probably think it was as funny as my drinking. Their affair was still at the stage where he was enchanted by everything She did. My headache was coming back, and I was glad to see Joseph loping through the yard, looking vague.

Being a dog of few words, Joseph nodded amiably at me and lay down to resume whatever nap he had interrupted elsewhere. I envied him. But before he could drift off, I asked whether he had happened to stop by my place. He thought for a while; I could tell he was thinking because of the way he blinked. Then he nodded. I asked if he had seen any mice. He thought some more and nodded again. Where had he seen the mice, I persisted. After it became apparent he could not quite recall, I suggested it might have been in the kitchen, since he usually makes a detour through that room just in case anything edible has been left out. Joseph nodded again, with an air of accomplishment.

Were they in the refrigerator? I asked, feeling as though I were pulling Joseph's molars with my bare paws. He thought again, and nodded gravely. Then I saw the blandness of his face dissolve into what, for Joseph, passed for animation. What is it? I asked before the thought became forever lost in the mists of his mind. The mice had left the refrigerator, Joseph disclosed in confidential tones. I sat up. That was the best news I'd received all afternoon, but my curiosity would not allow me to leave well enough alone. Did they say where they were going? I asked. Joseph considered for a while, then, miraculously, remembered. Something about back to the laboratory, he said. Evidently, the mental effort was telling on him, because he placed his paws over his head, a habit of his when he wanted to end a conversation, and one I have often been tempted to emulate.

I tried to relax and go to sleep, as I had wanted to do all day, but I kept thinking about Wilbur and

Christopher. It seemed to me an indictment of our society that two harmless mice had been driven back to a laboratory because human research had made it impossible for them to maintain normal lives in cozy holes in the wainscoting of houses. The more I thought about it the more indignant I became, and finally I woke up Joseph, who looked at me resentfully and asked what in the world was the matter. I told him, and he was silent, which was what I had expected; but he also was blinking rapidly.

After a long time, Joseph asked me what was so bad about a laboratory. I sputtered and asked if he had any idea of what animal experiments were and whether he had ever heard of vivisection. Joseph thought some more, while I noticed that dusk was beginning to fall and reflected that we might be bathed in moonlight before he opened his mouth again. Finally he said, well, everything was relative and he certainly didn't approve of vivisection, but some experiments were useful. From what he had gathered, said Joseph, an experiment had taught one of the mice how to live longer by taking naps in the cold, which was something he would like to know himself. And as far as the other mouse was concerned, by all accounts, if he hadn't been as bald as an egg, Rhinestone Cowcat would have eaten him on the spot. Joseph said he thought I need to be less emotional and think things through. Then he went back to sleep.

# Chapter 5

Reading the evening paper while I waited for her to come home, I was again exasperated by the amount of attention that the media pay to cats. In the middle of a perceptive piece about how pets can lower the blood pressure of people and what wonderful confidantes animals are, there was a lot of tickdiddle about something called the early interaction between people and kittens, which turned out to mean that you ought to pet pets, including cats. Regular handling, it said, would produce purry, people-oriented cats; as any dog can tell you, there's no such animal. Cats are the best actors in the world; with them, every purr has a purpose. Show me a cat that's affectionate for the sake of it, and I'll show you a cuddly werewolf. Not that they can't be warm and furry and all that—cats, I mean—but as I've often said to Joseph, look deep into a cat's eyes and what you see is contemplation of its next meal. Joseph always says it has never occurred to him to look deep into a cat's eyes.

According to what we read, there are about 48 million pet dogs, 27 million pet cats, and 25 million pet birds among the pet population in this country, so you can see which species ranks highest. And as far as caring for people is concerned, have you ever heard of a hearing-aid cat? How many cats do you know who have allowed themselves to be trained to leap up at the sound of a telephone or a door bell so they can alert their deaf owners?

How many seeing-eye cats have you run into at a traffic light? I suppose I shouldn't go on so about cats; Joseph says I'm becoming obsessive on the subject. But I have to admit my feeling that too much is made of them. What upsets me even more is the fact that She has bought a cat calendar, a set of those silly bed sheets and towels with cats in boots all over them, and a cat ashtray for Charlie. I suppose it was the ashtray that did it. He thinks cats are cute. I'm funny, in his opinion, but cats are cute. Whatever that's supposed to mean. He goes around the house reciting that peculiar poem about the cat who "loves to eat them mousies" and roaring with laughter. Which I suppose is another reason why he should have been the one to find the mice in the refrigerator. But I have the uneasy feeling he's getting to her about cats.

There was one awful moment when he asked if she'd ever thought of getting a cat to keep me company. Joe ought to have a pet cat of his own, he chortled. I couldn't resist a low growl, and She came over and ruffled the fur at the back of my head and said reproachfully, see, he'd upset me, and hadn't She told him I could understand every word they said. He went over and put his arm around her and said he hoped I couldn't understand *everything* they said to each other, and She gave that funny little embarrassed laugh she has now, and I stalked out into the yard. I could hear him sniggering behind my back and I wanted badly to bite him.

She ought to be home by now, but She isn't. Which I suppose means they're out to dinner, and if She gets back at all, it'll be a rerun of last night. And that oaf wonders why I drink? She brought home a book about a hundred ways to kill a cat, or skin a cat, I forget which, which seemed to be an attempt to mollify me, but I ignored it. Rhinestone Cowcat was insulted by it, but Terminal Hate thought it was pretty funny. He said it gave him some ideas for dull nights. And speaking of dull nights, this is turning out to be one of those. I had my dinner, and a martini or two, and felt a bit better. Joseph stayed for a while and told some stories. I enjoy Joseph when he tell stories, something he does very rarely.

You would never think it from his expression, but Joseph is a source of some remarkable animal lore. He says his father was a great storyteller before the bus got him. Some of his tales are rather gruesome, of course—like his account of something he calls the Tuolomne leg-bone and birch-bark tick, the only tick that eats holes in a perfect circle. According to legend, it was the leg-bone and birch-bark tick that chewed through Indian canoes in the early settlement days, and saved the white men whom the Indians were pursuing when their canoes sank.

Even more hair-raising are his stories about a horrid little thing called the San Joaquin Delta mesenteric belly-button worm, now fortunately believed to be extinct, who entered people's bodies through their navel or of the Dread Nubian nose bug who flew up the noses of dogs as well as people and consumed the gray matter behind the eyes so that the forehead fell in. (Now that I think of it, that might be just the solution for Charlie.) When I suggested that his father had made all this nasty stuff up, Joseph said he supposed I wouldn't believe in the existence of scamperdinks either. These, he said, were little crablike creatures who walked lopsided because they had nine legs, four on one side and five on the other, and that was why they were so easy to track. . . . He glimpsed the expression on my face and said, well, he supposed he had better get home as it was almost time for dinner and his owners always ate on time, unlike some he could mention.

I said I was always grateful for his company, although I had not found his conversation as edifying as usual, and Joseph sighed and said that in his opinion imagination was just as satisfying as alcohol. Then he left, and I went back to reading the paper, which I always scan for interesting items about dogdom. I came across an encouraging piece about some kindly folks in California who are putting together pet survival kits full of dehydrated health food so that we will all be able to live through Doomsday together. The stuff didn't sound too appetizing, but I do appreciate the thought.

I moved on from survival food to the animal-doctor column, which I always enjoy. It's sort of a dog's version of Dear Abby. I understand that Dr. Frank Miller, who writes the column from San Francisco, gets about ten thousand letters a year from pet owners seeking advice, and from the sound of the letters, God knows they need it. I do wish the good doctor would stop going on about canine alcoholics, though. One dog mentioned apparently began visiting bars with his owner and then took to drinking alone. I must say that She never takes me into bars with her, and most of the time I sip a martini merely to keep her company. But right now, I am still waiting for her, and if she gets to be much later, I may go out and see whether Dickens is around.

Dickens is a dog of considerable charm and wit, but he has no sense of direction at all and consequently spends a lot of his time getting lost, a flaw that accounts for the hours his owners spend wandering the neighborhood in their pajamas calling his name, not to mention the fact that the police have become so used to him they let him ride along for a while after they pick him up, because they know where he belongs, and they drop him off when it's convenient. Dickens says he gets to see a lot of things he would never see otherwise, and his only problem is that he worries about crossing streets.

# Chapter 6

I am back and She still isn't home, which makes it rather gloomy and chilly around the house, but I must say it was a lively evening. When I got over to Dickens' place, I discovered a great state of excitement. His owners were running around as if they'd had their heads cut off, and even Dickens, who has a pretty even disposition, probably as a result of all the time he spends not knowing where he is, seemed a bit shaken. It turned out that he had picked up a giant toad he found in the garden. Being Dickens and a kindly soul, he was merely being playful, of course, but the toad wasn't to know that. And what Dickens didn't know that I did because of my useful habit of reading the papers was that any dog who gets a mouthful of toad may expect to pass on quite soon to whatever is waiting in the next world. Toads are not my favorite animals, anyway. Personally I find frogs friendlier, but that's beside the point. Meanwhile, there was Dickens, having his mouth washed out, and I must say he is one of the few dogs I know who would put up with that kind of thing. Apparently he had dropped the toad before it poisoned him, but his owners couldn't be sure, although the fact that he was still alive might have told them something. They had called everybody from the veterinarian to the police.

Actually, since Dickens is never sick, the police know him a lot better than the veterinarian does, and they were quite intrigued by the whole thing. I gathered from the conversation that they were planning to stop by when they went off duty to see how he was. Dickens' owner said he would have to go out and buy more Scotch if the police were coming by when they were off duty, and did that dog have any idea how much he cost them in time and liquor and money, considering that he couldn't see what he was eating or where he was going and that he was practically being adopted by the local police precinct? Dickens' other owner, who was half drowning the poor dog by pouring warm water down his throat, said the poor darling couldn't help it if there were mean nasty toads in the backyard, could he?

She went off to heat more water, and Dickens looked at me and sighed. I asked if he wanted to come out for a little peaceful stroll and get away from all this madness, but he said, no, although he would like to, he thought he'd better not because his owners would have a heart attack if he left the house again that night. I asked what had happened to the giant toad, and he said it got the hell out of there as fast as it could. As far as he could tell, said Dickens, the toad was a lot more scared than he was. Personally speaking, he went on, he didn't think it would have done him any harm, especially as he had offered to give it a ride to where it was going after it had mentioned that it was lost. I said, a little incredulously, that it didn't seem to me to make much sense for Dickens to offer to take a toad anywhere when he never knew where he was going himself. Ah, said Dickens, this was different because the toad knew where it was going and it was giving him directions.

His owner returned at that point with another bowl of water and I left because I didn't like to watch a dog being treated like that, even if it was for his own good. On the way home, I noticed something stealthy in the shrubbery and when I saw an evil yellow eye peering over a bush, I nodded to Terminal Hate, who emerged to brag that he was on the track of interesting new prey. I asked what it was and he said a toad. Interesting, I said, and related to him the scene I had just witnessed at Dickens' house. Of course, Terminal Hate did not actually admit he had been wrong in his choice of dinner, but I noticed that some of the predatory glitter seemed to have faded from his eyes. I said I was sure that with a little patience he would find something else, and Terminal Hate said, "To quote the famous vulture on the branch, patience, hell, I want to go out and kill something."

I said I assumed that was his motto, and he preened a little and admitted that he felt he had done more than his share to distinguish his breed. I suggested it probably was all part of being owned by a former member of the United States Marine Corps, and Terminal Hate acknowledged that he had always been sorry about missing all the good wars. He would have enjoyed being a combat mascot, he confessed wistfully, and I assured him I was certain he would have been a credit to the regiment but not to despair, because from what I read in the newspapers, nuclear war was still a distinct possibility.

Terminal Hate shook his head. His owner, he said,

considered nuclear war a conflict without character—a bunch of scientists pushing buttons and depersonalizing the whole thing. His kind of war, said Terminal Hate, was hand-to-hand combat; something you could get your teeth into. I said it sounded pretty bloodthirsty to me and I would be just as happy without any war at all. Terminal Hate's lip curled and he said somebody had to be on top. I said I supposed that was so, and it was true nobody had managed to come up with anything more sensible so far, but one could always hope. Too many Nervous Nellies around, said Terminal Hate, in what I recognized as a direct quote from his owner. I said I expected my owner certainly qualified as one of those since She worried about killing a cockroach let alone going to war with Russia. Terminal Hate pointed out that She was a woman and what else could I expect? I replied a trace tartly that perhaps that kind of remark was why his owner had been divorced three times and was now living alone. Terminal Hate's whiskers bristled. His owner was not living alone, he said, unsheathing his formidable claws, his owner had him.

I apologized for what I realized was an inexcusable oversight and said I was sure I was keeping him from his night's work. Terminal Hate smiled, which in him is not a pleasant sight, and said there was a new dog on the block, one of those fancy poodles that spent all its time in the beauty parlor. He thought he might pay a call when it went out to do what its owner called its little poo-poo. I shuddered and wished him good night.

As I walked home through the dusk, I thought about my chat with Terminal Hate and how animals so often came to reflect their owners. Rhinestone Cowcat, for example, was owned by a woman who lived from one fad to the next, whether in clothes, food, politics, or health. She not only believed everything she read in the newspapers, but she promptly embraced it as her own. I could understand such behavior in a politician, but it always surprised me that people who weren't currying public favor could be so gullible. And I was sure that Rhinestone Cowcat's capacity for illogic, entertaining as it was from time to time, was directly traceable to her owner, whose platinum blonde hair had been red until she read in the paper that red dye caused cancer.

# Chapter 7

Well, I am not hungover this morning, but that's only because She and Charlie finished the gin, and he thought it would be just riotously funny to let me have only a splash. Abstinence, Joe, old boy, abstinence! he kept saying with that silly laugh of his, and I was very disappointed in her. She looked at me sort of apologetically at first, and then She said, well, maybe he does drink a little too much and I suppose it isn't good for him. She never worried about that before Charlie arrived, as I recall. In those days, She was grateful to have me to drink with. He really is beginning to get on my nerves. I feel so twitchy today, it's like having hangover symptoms without having had any of the fun, and if he hadn't been such a twit, I would have quite enjoyed the evening because they were talking about one of my favorite subjects—the problems of agriculture and bugs.

They had both been at the Med fly press conference and I noticed that amidst all their chatter there was not one word of understanding, let alone sympathy, for the insect or its problems. It's not that I found

Mame particularly appealing; as a matter of fact, she was self-centered enough to be a two-legged. It's the principle that troubles me, and I read about it all the time. Everything has to be the way people want it and, when you think about it, it's not as if people have done all that good a job. I wonder what it would be like if animals ran the world. I've never agreed with George Orwell's theories, which appear to be based on the concept that animals are prone to the same weaknesses as people. That may be true in that, of course, there are good and bad animals. But they are less subject to overwhelming vanity, which to my mind is the basis of the desire for human advancement. I lean more toward James Thurber's view of animals. He was savage about women and a lot of other things, but he was remarkably sagacious about creatures with four legs, or so I have always thought. All my ideas, of course, come from what I read, and I do try to read more than the papers, which is why She is always grumbling that the maid has jumbled up her books again. The maid watches television, which I despise, but I read. Sometimes She will read me something that has caught her attention in a newspaper or magazine or book, and I always listen attentively. She's forever telling people how I like her to read to me and how She is positive I understand every word. Then She kisses me on the top of my head, which I have learned to tolerate, although I prefer a good scratch.

Apparently, they had heard about Dickens' near mishap. Given the uproar his owners were making, it would have been hard for anyone with ears not to hear it. And She was worried that I might pick up a toad. Charlie said I looked as if I knew better than that, which raised him a bit in my estimation. But She said she worried about me because she was away so much and She was afraid I was lonely. Charlie said, somewhat sarcastically, that what I probably needed was a drink, and poured me a dollop of martini in a not-too-clean ashtray, which I thought was typical of his attitude toward me. But I drank it anyway.

At that point, She became coquettish, which tends to upset me, and said didn't She get a drink, too, and Charlie said absolutely and that wasn't all. It was about then that I decided it was time for me to scratch to be let out, since She doesn't know I can manipulate the kitchen-door catch by myself, and because I do not find demonstrations of affection among people very entertaining. Charlie got up and let me out—with alacrity, I might add—and I strolled around the backyard, feeling a little left out.

I try not to get depressed because, as owners go, She is quite presentable, and she gives me a great deal of freedom. But I couldn't help thinking how wonderful it would have been to see their expressions had they been able to hear my conversation with Mame. Or had Wilbur and Christopher still been asleep in the refrigerator when She opened it to get out the olives. She likes olives in her martinis, although speaking personally, I prefer onions.

I once broke the jar of olives in an effort to get her to change her habits but I mistimed it and had to live with the odor of olive juice all afternoon, not to mention her being extremely cross when She got home, and I didn't entirely blame her. She went straight out and bought another jar, too, so I gave up and am now trying to develop a taste for olives. Although, if old Charlie preferred onions, I bet she'd pick up a jar soon enough!

It was quiet in the backyard, but in the distance I could hear a hysterical yipping that I assumed meant

## *Chapter 7*

Terminal Hate had found the new poodle in town. I lay down on the grass, grateful for the mild evening, as I suspected nobody would remember to let me back in the house. I was almost asleep when I saw the rat, and I thought I must have been hallucinating, as I could have sworn it had a radio transmitter on its head. I blinked and looked again, and it *was* a rat with a radio transmitter. It looked at me gloomily and I could see why. It was a very small rat and even a transmitter that tiny had to be a bit of a load for it to cart around.

I asked it what had happened, and it sat down, fidgeting irritably at its transmitter, and said it was all the fault of vector control. I said it sounded like something out of science fiction and the rat said I was close. Humans, it explained, wanted to find out more about rats so they could exterminate them and, with the logic to be expected of humans, they wanted help from the rats. You mean somebody is listening in on that transmitter? I asked. The rat said it assumed so from what it had overheard when the thing was attached to its head. It added that the first time transmitters were tried it had turned out to be a real disaster, for both the radios and the rats.

I asked what had happened, and the rat said the vector control people had put its wired-up relatives in a garbage truck that turned out to be heading for a garbage compactor. I winced and the rat nodded.

It had heard the vector control chief discussing the whole thing, and the rat said he seemed annoyed at the loss of the transmitters. All that vector control had to say about the tragedy, it noted, was that it had been a helluva beep. Callous, I said. Indeed, agreed the rat. I asked if I could do anything to help remove the transmitter, and he gave me a rather peculiar look.

Why would he want to get rid of it? he asked. Feeling rather embarrassed, I said I just thought it might not be very comfortable to wear.

The rat said he appreciated my good intentions, but that as far as he was concerned, he was a part of history. I thought for a moment and told him he had a noble attitude. At that point we were interrupted by a shriek as She opened the kitchen door and saw not only me, but the rat. Apparently She missed the transmitter around its neck entirely, which shows you how observant She isn't, and saw only what She instantly decided was me being attacked by a huge vicious rat, as She put it.

The poor rat scurried off into the bushes, Charlie came charging out with a broom, and I wondered why people had to be so noisy. It all worked out quite well, however, because She was so upset at the idea that I might have been chewed up by a rat that She insisted on my sleeping at the foot of her bed, which I didn't mind at all, especially as it meant that Charlie went home. Sleeping with me was not what he had in mind.

# Chapter 8

Anyone in my world could tell you that all you have to do to know an earthquake is coming is to put your ear to the ground and really listen. If people paid more attention to animals, they would know a lot more about natural disasters. The other day, for example, She went off to cover what they call a moderate tremor that had damaged a small town, and since it was a long drive and She obviously wanted company, I went along. I thought it might be interesting because I would most likely meet friends who could tell me what had really happened.

Once we got there, it didn't seem to me it had been much of an earthquake; all that appeared to have been damaged was the local city hall, which may actually have been a godsend, considering what I have heard and read about local authority. But She had to talk to the mayor, who was just dying to be talked to, because the earthquake was the only reason anybody had ever wanted to talk to the little pipsqueak. He wouldn't allow dogs in even what was left of his office, however, so I sat down outside the building, wearing my good-patient-pet expression until She was safely inside, then I went to do a little investigative reporting of my own. I didn't have far to look. In the park down the street, I spotted an absolutely exhausted-looking snake, who was deep in conversation with an equally tired looking German shepherd. I introduced myself, and explained that I was just passing through while my owner wrote about the earthquake. The snake sighed so heavily his entire length shook.

"It was as plain as the nose on your face that it was coming," he said. "We tried to warn them. Quincy here—" nodding toward the German shepherd—"hasn't slept in ten days, I'm sure. The funny thing is that they know there's something wrong but they don't seem sharp enough to read the signs and they never seem to learn from one quake to another. It's really discouraging."

Quincy yawned. "I did all I could," he said. "I kept them awake three nights in a row trying to warn them, pawing the ground, digging things up in the backyard, howling. How they could have ignored me, I don't know."

"They didn't ignore you," said the snake. "They locked you in the backyard and complained about the noise you were making. Said they couldn't sleep."

"They really don't listen, do they?" I commented sadly. I was lying down so that I could better hear the snake, whose voice was wispy with fatigue.

"Listen?" said the snake wearily. "The sky would have to fall before they paid attention, and then they'd probably say it was the Russians." He quivered a little in the grass—"You can still hear it."

We were all quiet for a few minutes, and I could easily sense and hear the shuddering and groaning of the earth beneath me, indicating that the so-called moderate earthquake had not yet quite done with the town. I wondered how long She was going to spend with the mayor, who looked as if the sense in his head wouldn't fill a matchbook cover, and whether I should go and get her. But that would only get the mayor grumbling about her dog, and her grumbling to me about how I interfered with her work.

"How much more do you think?" I asked the snake, who seemed about to doze off.

"Not much. It's just sort of hiccuping now," he said. "You should have been here yesterday."

"Like sitting on top of a volcano," said Quincy. "My pads are still blistered."

"That was from all the rushing around you did," said the snake. "Not that you got any gratitude for it. Even when their entire back wall cracked. And that house is so flimsy the roof could have come in."

"That was what worried me," said Quincy. "I usually sleep with the child in that back bedroom."

The snake stretched himself in the sun. "It's fascinating," he said thoughtfully. "They have gadgets to gauge the movement of the earth. They work at figuring out tension in rocks and changes in magnetic fields and whether the slope of the land is changing. Creepmeters and tiltmeters and strainmeters and detectors all over the place. But it never occurs to them that animals, who are closer to natural phenomena, would logically know such things first. Why don't they wonder why a cock is crowing at three in the afternoon and the horses are having hysterics, or folks like me are crawling hell-bent out of what for us is usually safe ground." He shook his head and tail at the same time.

I said I had read somewhere that they had decided to watch us too.

The snake sniffed. "If we stood up on our hind legs, so to speak, and told them what we know in language they could understand," he said, "they'd either lock us up for special tests or shoot us for fear that we knew more than they did."

"As if we could know any less," said Quincy. "Even that dumb canary that belongs to my owner's daughter was acting like a maniac. Cheeped day and night and practically beat out whatever brain it's got against its cage door. What did they do? Gave it aspirin."

I shook my head sympathetically.

"Of course," said the snake, "when the big one comes, then it won't matter what they do, because we'll be gone. Every animal in its right mind will head out of town to open country, and if people had any sense, they'd realize we weren't leaving on vacation."

"This wasn't too bad, though?" I asked.

The snake shook its head. "Nothing like the one in L.A. in—when was that? Seventy-one? That one had promise. They were lucky with that one. I have friends down there—some of your people, in fact, Quincy, who've just been nervous wrecks ever since."

Quincy nodded. "When he realized it was a big one, my cousin Rex," he said, "went straight through a screen door they were stupid enough to have locked. He said that seemed to upset them more than the quake."

I heard a faint but familiar cry in the distance and got to my feet.

"Yours a writer?" asked the snake, writhing lazily.

I nodded. "She's a reporter for *The World.*"

"And she's talking to the mayor, of course?"

"I'm afraid so," I said. "She said the town government was complaining about lack of preparedness."

"A wonderful phrase. Wonderful. Sort of like supply-side preparedness," said the snake, and closed his eyes.

"Well, thanks for giving me the facts."

"Too bad you can't publish them," said Quincy.

They were both already asleep as I padded back to the car where She was calling my name and looking impatient.

"Where have you been? I was worried about you," She said, which did not displease me. I clambered into the car beside her, and She told me the mayor was a fool, which I thought was reassuringly perceptive. We drove off to talk to some people who could tell her what it had felt like when the floors heaved and the pictures fell off the walls. Then one man mentioned how oddly his dog had been behaving for the past week.

"Really?" She said.

He nodded. "Usually the best behaved beast you ever saw, and he's been raising hell for days. Howling, pawing holes in the rugs, digging up half the rose bed. Like he was trying to tell us something."

I uttered what She calls my whiffling sound, which I think is the equivalent of somebody in her world clearing his throat, and She glanced sharply at me.

"Maybe he was," She suggested to the man, who chuckled.

"Sure. Maybe he was. More like a touch of distemper."

# Chapter 9

When we got home, She went back to her office to write her story, and I knew She'd probably meet him afterward and that would mean She wouldn't be home until late and I'd be alone again. I wasn't sure how much gin was left, so I decided to take a stroll over by the zoo, which is one of my favorite places. I go to the zoo the way people stop off at a bar. You get a wide range of conversation and quite a bit of animal interest when creatures are caged. Today was no exception. Everybody seemed depressed when I wandered in. They don't pay much attention to me now, although the keepers used to get a bit nervous until they realized I was simply taking a walk, minding my own business, and was not about to molest their charges.

I find zoo keepers, on average, more sensitive to how my world thinks than people on the outside. It has filtered into their minds that there may be more to an animal than four feet and fur. Some of them even seem to have reached the point where they realize you don't always have to talk to understand somebody. But as I said, things were very low there today. Even

Kola the tiger was subdued, and she is usually so disdainful of her surroundings she wouldn't notice if someone made off with her coat. I asked what was wrong and she said it was poor Jewel.

Jewel the hippopotamus? I asked, and she said the only other jewel she knew was the one that woman on the board of directors kept flashing on her finger. Kola can be rather snappish, so I didn't ask her anything else, although I could see she was itching to tell. Instead, I headed for the hippo enclosures, leaving her frustrated, I'm sure.

The atmosphere was certainly funereal over there. Jewel's keeper was trying to tempt her to eat, and when I noticed it was a pail of vanilla ice cream, which is her great weakness, I knew things were bad. Jewel was standing in her wading pool looking as miserable as I have ever seen a hippopotamus look. I whiffled a bit, and she glanced over at me and nodded. I said I had heard she wasn't doing so well and I was sorry to hear it. Jewel sighed a sigh that almost blew her keeper into the pool, and said I wouldn't be doing so well either in her situation. I sat down and asked if it would help to talk about it, and she said, well, to begin with, had I heard that Vanderbilt was dead? I was shocked; Vanderbilt was Jewel's mate and as decent and easygoing a hippo as any I'd met. It turned out that he had been too easygoing. As Jewel told it, some visitors had been throwing a ball to one another and Vanderbilt, feeling playful, perhaps because he was about to become a father, had caught the ball in his mouth.

He choked? I asked in horror. It was a big ball, said Jewel grimly. But it wasn't so much that he choked as that the ball was just too big for even Vanderbilt's internal mechanism to deal with. By the time the keepers realized it was a crisis, it was too late. He died, said Jewel, on the operating table. I offered my condolences, and, hoping to cheer her up, said that at least she would have the baby to take her time up. I hadn't heard everything, said Jewel in tomb-like tones.

I waited. I was beginning to be sorry I had asked. Jewel absently slurped up some ice cream, to the joy of her keeper, and said she had become a mother the day after Vanderbilt died. Yes? I said, encouragingly. Jewel contemplated her keeper, who was urging her to eat more ice cream, and I had the feeling she had spent too much time listening to elderly visitors regaling each other with lurid accounts of their last operation. I had to realize, said Jewel, that she had been distraught over Vanderbilt's death. It had come as a terrible shock to her. I knew, she said, how devoted they had been. I didn't know that I would have used the word devoted to describe a couple whose fights had the sound and fury of medieval jousting, but it was no time to dispute her matrimonial imagery. Indeed, I said. Then, said Jewel, I could understand that her mind was preoccupied. Yes, I said cautiously, I could understand that. It was becoming clear that Jewel was carefully paving the way for an admission she would have preferred not to make, and I was beginning to fear I knew what it was.

Summoning up my reserves of tact, I said I expected that, in the circumstances, the birth of the baby must have been traumatic for her. Jewel nodded vigorously, causing her keeper, who assumed she was still hungry, to shovel in more ice cream. Jewel swallowed, smacked her lips, and resumed her doleful tale. It had been the night after the baby was born, she related. She had been thinking about Vanderbilt and how she was now alone in the world.

I nodded, noticing that my left hind paw had gone to sleep. Her eyes had been clouded by tears, said Jewel, an assertion I greeted with silence. The baby, she continued after a pause, had been curled up close by her. It was then, said Jewel, that it happened. What happened? I asked before she could embellish the scene any further. She must have dozed off, said Jewel, no doubt out of emotional and physical exhaustion. And she had rolled over. Rolled over? I asked. Jewel nodded. Rolled over, she said. And the baby? I asked. Jewel closed her tiny beady eyes as though the subject were too painful to think about, let alone discuss, and it was unfortunate that at that moment her keeper, standing dutifully by with the bucket of ice cream, was asked by a passer-by about the hippo tragedy. The keeper was a young man who put things succinctly.

"Squashed," he said clearly. "Squashed it like a bug."

"Poor little thing," said the visitor.

Jewel looked offended.

What about me? she demanded indignantly. She was the one who had done most of the suffering, she pointed out. First Vanderbilt and that damned ball, and then she had sat on her only child. She was the one who deserved sympathy. I said she certainly did and took my departure while she was grumbling about people's lack of sensitivity. When I looked back, she was repeating the whole story to the zebra next door and was well into her second bucket of ice cream.

# Chapter 10

Any time you run into a dog with three legs who says he's been out looking for eggs, it's a good reason for getting home late. It was almost dusk when I left the zoo. I was hoping She might be home, even if he was with her, and that they'd have stopped at the liquor store on the way, so I was hurrying along when I noticed this rather odd-looking German shepherd mix, sitting on the sidewalk scratching his nose. As I went by I heard him cursing to himself, so I stopped, being compassionate as well as possessed by curiosity, and asked if I could do anything to help. He stopped scratching long enough to look at me rather pitifully. It was those damned moth hairs, he said. I begged his pardon and asked if I had heard him correctly? Damned right, said the dog. Had I ever had moth hairs up my nose?

I said, not to my recollection and it was nothing I would want to experience. He said, well, in that case I should be grateful I was a sheltered house pet, as my polished leather collar seemed to indicate, and not a dog that had found itself forced by circumstances to spend its life looking for moth eggs. I said I had never heard of such a thing, and he said neither had anybody else who was in their right mind. It was the gypsy moths, he explained, scratching as he spoke. They were infesting half the country, half the world for all he knew, and it was very difficult to find their eggs.

I said I was sorry, but my knowledge of gypsy moths was decidedly limited, and the dog said he didn't blame me for that. He personally had barely heard of them until he found that his tracking skills had qualified him to be part of a canine egg-hunting unit. Did I, he asked, know what gypsy moths did with their eggs? I said I didn't. He had to admit they were quite crafty, said the dog, whose nose appeared to be puffy, whether from scratching or moth hairs it was difficult to say. What they did, he said, was to coat the egg clusters with their own hair, then glue them to some convenient tree trunk, which meant that when the eggs hatched, the caterpillars had dinner on the table, as it were. They ate the tree? I asked. The dog made an impatient sound; they ate the leaves, he said. One hungry little caterpillar could wolf down a square foot of leaves in a day, so he supposed I could imagine what thousands of hungry little caterpillars would do to a tree. I said I had noticed some of the trees looking a bit moth-eaten, and he nodded.

Moth-eaten was right, he said. The agricultural people were going nuts because they couldn't find those eggs sticking to the trees, so of course they had to call on those who could. Like dogs, I said, with quiet pride. Like dogs, he said. And they had found them? I asked. Well, of course, they had found the eggs, said the dog, why the hell did I think he was scratching his nose like that? Moth hairs, I said. Up his nose. Precisely, said the dog. To find the eggs, they had to use their noses, and those goddamned moth hairs were the hardest things to get off his nose he had ever encountered since the night he had inadvertently slept on somebody's mohair blanket.

I suggested that scratching might not be the answer. The dog said, no doubt I was right but did I have any better ideas? How about cold water? I asked. Bathing his nose in it, I meant. He said he hadn't thought of that but it might be a good idea. He was going to have to find something to get rid of those hairs or else he was going to be spending more time scratching his nose than egg-hunting. What about the other dogs in the unit? I asked. They were in better shape, he said, because he had led the way. When you have only three legs and everybody else has four, said the dog, you have to be proving yourself all the time, so of course he had found more eggs than anybody else and he had found them first. I said I thought that was pretty commendable and he said it was a damned bore, especially since he could operate as well as anybody; it was just a question of getting used to the balance thing. But humans were always crooning over him and making a great fuss, so he got a lot of perks and maybe it had all been worth it.

I ventured to ask how he had lost the leg, and the dog swaggered a little, which wasn't easy to do when he was still scratching his nose. The biggest mastiff you ever saw, he said. Leg got so chewed up the vet just had to take it off. Nothing else to be done. I made sounds of admiration, and looked up to see a man in a leather jacket come strolling down the road.

"Hey Bart," said the man. "You still having trouble with that nose?" The dog looked at him reproachfully. "They're great for stating the obvious," he remarked to me.

The man scratched behind the dog's ears.

"We'd better get you over to the vet in case that's an allergy you're developing to those damned eggs," he said. The dog sat down firmly in the road.

"Come on," said the man. "You like the vet. You remember him. You've known him since you were a pup. Matter of fact, he was the one who saved your life—nobody thought a dog born with three legs would live, but he pulled you through. Come on—he'll fix you right up."

The dog didn't look at me, and I said nothing. Watching him hop away with the man in the leather coat, I decided I couldn't blame him for his little fiction. If you had to go through life with three legs, you might as well make it an ego trip. Then I decided I might as well go home. The combination of Jewel's troubles and the moth eggs had unsettled my stomach and I felt in need of a little pick-me-up.

My spirits dropped when I found Charlie sitting with his feet up on the coffee table and his arm around her, but to my surprise, he acted quite human, for a human. He gave me a very satisfactory scratch around the ears and hips and said, hey, old fellow, you look depressed, you look like you need a drink.

I was so astounded, I wagged my tail at him, which may have been overdoing it, but I have always been one to respond in kind. He poured my drink into one of her best crystal bowls instead of the usual ashtray, which made her laugh, and made me wonder if maybe I'd been misjudging him after all. I don't mean I've changed my mind about him, but maybe he was nervous about me, too. I mean, I suppose I should be flattered She is so obviously fond of me that he considered me competition. Anyway, after my second bowl of martinis, I went so far as to lean my head on his knee, and he seemed downright delighted.

# Chapter 11

Sometimes I think animals are becoming more and more like people. I discovered recently that there is an adopted burro living in the neighborhood, the only burro living around here that I ever heard of—I didn't know anybody had a yard big enough to keep one. I've been reading a lot about burros, because She's been writing a lot about them. She was in the Mojave desert a while back writing about how they're chewing up the desert and all the environmentalists want them to be removed because man brought them there during the prospecting days and man ought to remove them, which, as usual, entirely ignores the position of the burros, who've been around the desert for maybe fifty years and have just as much right to live there as the environmentalists, who may, incidentally, be less in tune with Mother Nature than they seem to think they are.

However, there do appear to be an awful lot of burros around. The solution people have come up with is either to put them up for adoption or to shoot them, which isn't much of a choice for the burro. She doesn't seem to have heard about our neighborhood burro, but then She is like most people, I am sorry to say, and doesn't hear about almost anything until it comes up and bites her on the leg, so to speak.

Since She didn't take me to the desert with her and just as well, judging by her description of it when She got back, and since I had never met a burro, I thought I'd just stop by and welcome him or her to the neighborhood. I found him with the help of Terminal Hate, who keeps an eye on everything that moves, in case he thinks it's worth attacking, and trotted over there to be friendly. The burro, who said his name was Burt, looked exceedingly well fed, to the point of being almost comatose, and I judged that his adoptive owners were trying to make up for his being unwanted; the poor-little-thing-let's-take-care-of-it-whether-it-wants-it-or-not syndrome I call it. Burt said he really wasn't accustomed to this kind of gluttony and didn't people ever do anything except go to the market and then eat what they brought home? I said it seemed to be an obsession with most of the ones I knew, but at least it had to be better than being hunted down in the desert by a posse.

Burt got a nostalgic look in his eye that puzzled me, and said, well, it hadn't been all that bad. He liked being shot at? I asked. Burt said, not exactly, but it certainly had made his days exciting. There was never a dull moment in those days, he said, it was sort of like being an outlaw in the Old West. He had, he said, been watching television with the son of his new owners, who was addicted to cowboy movies, and just seeing all that sagebrush and cactus and open country had made him a bit homesick.

I suggested it was probably a matter of nostalgia, now that he was safe, but Burt said, no, when he looked around at this dinky little yard with nowhere to go and nothing to do but eat, he really missed the old days. One of the problems, he said, was that the people who had adopted him had been told that burros ate anything and that was what they fed him. Pizza, potato chips, hot dogs, hamburgers, ice cream, French fries, chocolate-chip cookies—it was a wonder he could stand up, let alone run away, which was what they apparently worried about, from what he had overheard. I asked why he didn't just refuse to eat it so that maybe they'd give him healthier food. Burt said he had been brought up to eat what was put in front of him and even what wasn't put in front of him, and he didn't feel secure enough yet to get picky.

Aha, I said, so he was anxious to stay after all, despite all his mooning after his old lifestyle. Burt said he was anxious to go on getting fed, wherever he was, and he certainly couldn't complain of mistreatment. They had even been willing to let him sleep indoors, mostly because the child wanted it, but he had made clear his preference for sleeping in the fresh air, or what remained of it after the cars had clogged it up. He certainly did miss the desert atmosphere, and also the peace and quiet. People didn't talk so much in the wide-open spaces, he said, a touch pointedly I thought. I said I was sorry for taking up so much of his time and Burt said, no, no, he was glad to talk to somebody with some sense. At least I had some idea of what he was talking about, even though I was obviously an urban animal. I didn't think I liked the sound of that too much and informed him I considered myself very well informed about our world and theirs.

Burt said he was sure I was, but I had never had to take care of myself, had I? I admitted reluctantly that that was so, although I felt I could do a perfectly good job if I had to. Maybe so, maybe so, said Burt, but he would still like to see me survive in his kind of country, with bullets flying past my head. I said I supposed you could adjust to just about anything if you had to, and Burt said that was the point he was making, that he had really adjusted to being sort of like Jesse James—he obviously had been watching a lot of television, I reflected—and on the run day and night. It gave life a fine cutting edge, he said, with a wistfulness I found faintly ridiculous. I said that if he really wanted to go back, I expected his owners would oblige him if he acted unhappy enough. Burt waggled his ears at me and said he wasn't unhappy, it was just that he got a little bored from time to time, especially when his day seemed to be one long dinner. A lot of animals would like to have his problem, I remarked tartly, and Burt nodded. He was sure that was true, he said, and he was prepared to make the best of things.

He had heard his owners say, he went on, that he was such a wonderful pet for little William that their neighbors up the street were considering forking out the seventy-five dollars, or whatever the current going rate was, for a burro for their little girl. That would be nice, said Burt, because it would probably be one of his friends or relatives and with any luck it would be a female burro. He obviously had his future all mapped out, I commented, and think of the stories he could tell his children about the days when burros roamed the West.

Burt said he couldn't have put it better himself, but I would have to excuse him because he had to go indoors. He'd heard there was a rerun of *Shane* on television, and he was just dying to see it. Besides which, he was a little peckish and William always had Snickers bars while he watched old movies, not to mention a little homemade popcorn. I said I didn't think he'd be able to outrun his pursuers if he did go back to the desert. Burt heaved himself to his feet, considered his ample girth, and said maybe I had something there. Then he waddled into the house.

I went on about my business, reflecting gloomily on the infinite range of corruption. Instead of being shot, Burt would probably die a premature death from high blood pressure and obesity. Which made me reflect that my own situation was a vast improvement on his. If I had to depend on any human, mine was a lot better than most, and considerably more intelligent. And in view of that fact I admitted reluctantly that if She were as fond of Charlie as She seemed to be, perhaps I ought to have second thoughts about him myself. No matter who came along, She would certainly always need me. And it was possible that I might be able to train Charlie to become more civilized. I hoped I wasn't leaning too far toward giving him the benefit of all my doubts, but he was nice to her, and I had to admit that was what mattered, because when She was unhappy, it placed a tremendous burden on me, not to mention tripling my drinking and hers. Moreover, Charlie had been downright friendly the last day or so. And he hadn't even laughed when I tripped over my martini bowl on the way to bed.

# Chapter 12

She said I disgraced her today, but I take the position that in my world dignity must be maintained, and while I have no objections to a friendly scratch behind the ears or a good rubdown along the sides, I am not about to subject myself to the dubious pleasures of a pet massage parlor. And that is where She took me, in the interests of what She insisted was a great feature story for *The World.* I would have been the laughingstock of *my* world if I had submitted to the indignities they had in mind. To begin with, the place was decorated in what appeared to be Reynolds Wrap, with inset photographs of animals in what I considered ludicrous positions, and neon lights across the ceiling. Poochie's Parlor, it was called, which is enough to make any self-respecting animal throw up.

She said She had heard about the importance of massaging your pet, and She thought it would be great fun to see how I liked it. She said she had always respected my opinion. Well, She got it, and now Poochie's Parlor is saying it's going to sue her and *The World* for some absurd amount of money. They say I ruined their wall-to-wall purple carpeting, which I trust is true, chewed a doggie vibrator to pieces, and bit the owner who, apart from anything else, had hands like dead fish.

When I arrived, the owner, with visions of free publicity dancing in his shiny, bald head, was all over me, and She knew my reaction immediately because all the fur at the back of my neck was standing on end. I was such a gorgeous, gorgeous fellow, said this cretin, such noble bearing, and just look at those hindquarters. Well, I'll tell you, nobody is going to look at my hindquarters in that tone of voice, if you know what I mean. As far as I know, I have perfectly adequate hindquarters, or at least I had no complaints from that dishy retriever who used to live three blocks away and who may be a mother by now, for all I know —and I am certainly no prude. But if animals and people are going to get along, there has to be a certain degree of reserve, and the owner of Poochie's Parlor overstepped it.

He told her I was practically their first customer, and the way things went, I may have been their last. While She was taking notes, and trying not to giggle, he was taking liberties, and finally I did what any dog would have had to do. I sank my teeth tidily into his wrist, which had the result of instantly removing his hand from the hindquarters that seemed to hold such a fascination for him. I've read about people like him, but I thought they kept them locked up, or at least with their own kind. Well, the uproar that followed that almost made the trip worthwhile, and in my view it made her story a great deal better reading because it told animal owners just what to expect.

She said I was a naughty boy, which is not what She says when She is really furious with me. She usually throws something at me, which I regard as normal behavior for people who don't have any teeth worth mentioning. Peter of Poochie's Parlor said I was a vicious brute and ought to be put to sleep immediately, and I was probably rabid. She said he was exaggerating the whole thing; his wrist wasn't even bleeding, at least not much, and in any case what had he been doing to me to make me do such a thing, because normally I was a dog of sweet and gentle disposition who had never bitten anyone in his whole life. Which was a lie, of course, as some of her former boyfriends could attest. Peter said he was going to call his lawyer right there and then and it would cost *The World* a million dollars and she could say goodbye to that monster, because he was going to have the police pick it up at once. She said he was welcome to call his lawyer, but she didn't think he would get very far with a case against a dog who had reacted because he was having what anybody would recognize as lewd advances made to him.

Peter practically had apoplexy and said how dare she, and She said that in addition to taking notes, She had had her tape recorder on and the playback of what he had been saying to her dog would certainly make interesting reading. He said that if she didn't leave his premises, he would have us both arrested, and She said maybe She should stay and warn other customers, or would he rather they read about it in *The World*?

Peter said, well, he would put a Band-Aid on his wrist, maybe he had pinched me a little, unintentionally, of course, and She said, very coolly, maybe he had but, in any case, She would be happy to describe his premises and what he was offering for the readers of *The World*. Peter said, why didn't She sit down and read his pamphlet about pet massage while he made them both a cup of coffee and maybe her—he choked a little there—dog would like some water? She said She would take any material he had, but She didn't care for any coffee and She was sure her dog didn't care for any water either. She ostentatiously clipped on the leash She almost never uses, presumably so Peter couldn't claim that I was running around wild, and stalked out. I must say it wasn't a bad performance for her, even though She did put me through a rather sordid experience.

Her story was really pretty good. She said She wished I could read it, although you'd think that from the attention I pay to the papers, it would be fairly obvious that I understood them. Of course I did read it, and She did quite a job on Peter and his Poochie parlor, although it was nicely tongue-in-cheek and I expect *The World's* lawyers took a look at it to be sure he wouldn't have any more grounds for suing than he already had. I read it as soon as She put the paper down, and afterward I went over to her and gave her a good lick on the nose, which is something I very rarely do since I consider it a little too puppyish. She looked at me with the funniest expression and said she believed I had really read her story. I was so surprised at her perception that I licked her on the nose again.

# Chapter 13

I usually enjoy going along on her trips, although it seems to me we always get different sides of the story. Last weekend She was working on a piece about the national forests, and what is happening to the sequoias, so we packed a picnic hamper with a nice Thermos of martinis in it, and took off. Charlie had to meet with one of his clients, so he couldn't come along, and she invited me instead. I was pleased, of course, although I have to admit he and I are sort of adjusting to each other and he does give really exhilarating rubdowns. She is very affectionate with me, always scratching my ears and brushing my coat, which I enjoy, but Charlie has turned out to have a good strong touch, which may be one of the reasons She likes him, too. Anyway, I have always prided myself on being fair, and there have been moments recently when I've felt I wouldn't mind having Charlie around all the time. He doesn't laugh at me any more when I have a martini; I make what you might call a dignified fuss when he arrives, and I must say he does seem to appreciate the attention.

But it was nice to have her to myself again. She chatters away to me while we drive, which She always seems to enjoy, because She says I look so attentive and I never disagree with her. Anyway, once we got into the forest area, She found the usual swarm of park rangers and forest service officials and I, as usual, strolled off into the trees, which didn't bother the people, as they assumed it was for a purpose other than conversation.

There was a car parked near hers, and as I went by it, I heard the oddest crunching sound, almost as if somebody were eating inside the hood. I stopped and sniffed, and I became certain that somebody *was* eating something inside the hood of what was a pretty expensive foreign car, presumably left there by tourists who were off admiring all those great big trees. I moved closer to the car and saw that the hood was partially open. I peered through the aperture and the chomping stopped, but I could see a furry shape inside, and as my eyes became accustomed to the oily gloom, I saw it was a marmot with some wire dangling from its mouth. It stared at me in a rather offended manner, and I said I was sorry if I had disturbed it, but it was a little unusual to hear somebody eating inside the hood of a car.

The marmot scampered over to the edge of the hood, swallowing the remains of whatever portion of the car's mechanism it had been chewing on, and said, well, everybody had to eat somewhere, and this was where its food was. I said I had never heard of a marmot eating cars, and the marmot said it didn't eat the whole car, of course, just the chewy parts, like wiring and rubber. Really quite tasty, it said, and cars like this Alfa-Romeo were the most flavorful. I asked if it had always preferred cars' innards for dinner, and the marmot said, no, it had started out on rubber boots and backpacks, but the boots were now made of a much tougher rubber and weren't nearly as juicy.

I asked if that kind of thing weren't difficult to digest, and the marmot said, not really, when you considered what it was accustomed to eating, and the important thing was that it had to stock up in the summer so it could have a good winter's nap. I said I realized that, but I was surprised that car rubber was so digestible on a long-term basis. Plastic insulation was good, too, volunteered the marmot, picking a fragment of wire out of its teeth; it seemed to work like vitamins, gave you a lot of stamina. I said that was very interesting, but didn't it result in complaints from the owners of the cars? Indeed, yes, said the marmot, recalling with considerable relish one engine it had eaten so much of that when the driver turned the key in the ignition, the entire system went up in smoke, so to speak, and the car had to be towed to the nearest garage. The marmot said it would have given a lot to have been there when the mechanics opened the hood and found the charred remains.

But it had to be careful it didn't get caught, it mentioned. I said I could imagine that car owners would be anything but pleased to find their cars were on a marmot's menu. The marmot nodded. There was one time it got carried away, chewing on a really delicious piece of rubber hose while the owner started the car and drove off. It hadn't disturbed the marmot too much, it said; in fact, it had simply eaten faster so as not to leave anything, and finally the driver had noticed water pouring from the engine.

His expression when he opened the hood, said the marmot, was something it would laugh over all winter. I looked nervously back down the road toward her car and asked if it would be kind enough to make an exception now and again. The marmot followed my glance and asked if that was my owner's car? Not to worry, it said, it certainly wouldn't want to get me stranded in the woods with someone who looked as if She wouldn't know how to open the hood, let alone catch a marmot. I thanked it and wished it a nice winter's sleep, and when I got back to the car, She was chatting with a tall ranger who was telling her that at this count, they've chewed up eleven cars and a fire truck. I smiled to myself and got into the car to wait for her. She was full of her story, and on the way back she couldn't wait to tell me about those awful little yellow-bellied marmots who were gobbling up people's cars.

I listened to her for a while, and then began to paw at the hamper on the floor. Although I am not about to be critical of what other animals eat, I know what I like, and to my mind, a nice rare hamburger and a good splash of martini are a great deal tastier than a pair of rubber boots.

# Chapter 14

I have sometimes wondered what would be considered justification for homicide in my world. What put the thought into my head was a story Terminal Hate told me. He said it illustrated the native stupidity of dogs, but I knew that he was really just trying to pick an argument, so I pointed out to him that cats were equally vulnerable to that kind of indignity. I should explain that what he was talking about was this new so-called spiral cut they are inflicting on poodles, who, God knows, already have enough to put up with in terms of what their owners do to their fur. Poodles are intelligent animals, and I have known some who went through life in a state of perpetual embarrassment not to mention perpetual colds because half of them was covered in fur and half of them was naked skin. This spiral cut Terminal Hate described with such glee makes a dog look like a screw on a leash, as one perceptive observer described it, since the fur is clipped in a narrow spiral from head to tail.

Terminal Hate said he had met a poodle with a

spiral cut. Not only that, he noted, but its owner had dyed the silly dog a sort of reddish color that made it look as if it had been left out in the rain to rust. In all his years of dog-watching, said Terminal Hate with satisfaction, he had never seen such a spectacle. Where, he demanded, would I find a cat allowing itself to look that ridiculous? No wonder cats had taken over the best-seller list. People had finally realized how much more intelligent they were.

I said that was a vile canard, even for him, and the only reason people paid any attention at all to cats was because they were supposed to be good at ridding houses of what people considered pests like mice and rats, although some cats I knew seemed to have let their killer instinct run away with them. Terminal Hate said a cat had to do what a cat had to do, and he had to protect his turf. From what? I asked. From trespassers, he answered nastily. I said that wasn't the point; the point was what people were allowed to do to animals. Animals like dogs, Terminal Hate reiterated. He knew of no cat with a spiral cut, he said firmly, because any cat's owner who tried to give it one would wind up with a faceful of claw, which was how it should be.

What about cat shows? I asked, somewhat feebly, since it was true that I had never seen a member of Terminal Hate's species subjected to the kind of public humiliation that some dogs tolerated. So cats were in shows, said Terminal Hate. The worst anyone ever did to them was to put a ribbon around their neck, and any cat worth its claws would make short work of that. Dogs, on the other hand, were apparently willing to put up with any ignominy people chose to inflict on them. How did I account for this deplorable weakness of character? I couldn't and didn't. I knew Terminal Hate would only sneer if I suggested that dogs put up with such miseries out of affection for their owners and not out of weak-mindedness, as he was suggesting.

The fault lay with people, I contended. This was just one more illustration of what they were capable of in their decadence. Terminal Hate said, humph, it was no more than an illustration of how wishy-washy dogs were. What about Rhinestone Cowcat's collar? I asked waspishly. Terminal Hate fidgeted a little and demolished a rose bush with his left front claw. Rhinestone Cowcat was a female, he said finally, and not able to stand up for her rights the way he was. Nonsense, I said, seizing on the chink in his argument. I knew that he personally had trained Rhinestone Cowcat in the feline martial arts, and she was perfectly capable of slicing her owner's fingers to the bone if she so chose. Terminal Hate muttered sulkily that he was not responsible for Rhinestone Cowcat's choosing to act like a female; he had done the best he could for her. It had nothing to do with her being female, I said; he always fell back on that argument when he couldn't think of anything else.

What the hell did it have to do with, then? demanded Terminal Hate. Rhinestone Cowcat knew it pleased her owner to have her wear that silly collar, I said. Terminal Hate refused to go along with that. Why else would she wear it, then, I asked. If cats were as smart and aggressive as he said they were, Rhinestone Cowcat certainly could have lost the collar long ago, or simply refused to have it buckled on her. At least she didn't look like a corkscrew, said Terminal Hate defensively. I acknowledged that she didn't, but insisted that she wore the collar out of affection for her owner, just as those unfortunate poodles allowed themselves to be clipped out of affection for their owners.

Terminal Hate said I was being soppy as usual, and he was not going to waste his time on any more of these silly philosophical discussions I liked so much. As far as he was concerned, cats were free spirits and dogs were sycophants and people had finally realized it. I said one characteristic cats shared with their owners was their insensitivity. The kind of people who owned cats . . . I began. Terminal Hate said, just a minute, nobody was going to say anything about his owner while he was around. Oh, I said, I thought he was a free spirit who didn't care about anyone, and what if his owner decided to get him a nice shiny collar? Terminal Hate said if it weren't that he'd known me so long and was convinced I was harmless he'd take my eye out, and he stalked into the shrubbery.

I can't say I was sorry to see him go, because while you rarely win an argument with Terminal Hate, you never win a fight with him, although I must admit I haven't tried in years and don't plan to. But I kept thinking about that poor poodle who looked like a corkscrew and it made me feel quite kindly toward my owner. I was willing to bet that poodle's owner never thought of giving it a drink, even after abusing it so outrageously, and that made me reflect on my own cozy domestic situation. I never imagined I would say this, but once or twice in the past day or so, I have actually thought Charlie made more sense than She did. He's certainly more logical. And when he looked over at me the other night and said, I bet Joe agrees with that, I found myself wagging my tail quite enthusiastically, even if She was giving me a downright reproachful look. She was very attentive later, but I kept in mind how she had ignored me when Charlie first came to stay, and it occurred to me that she just might be playing games with both of us. Anyway, Charlie and I shared a martini and She went off to bed.

# Chapter 15

I thought this morning that we had been invaded, but it turned out to be just a troop of Boy Scouts chasing snails. She was as annoyed as I was because She is not a morning person either and, as She said, all She needs on top of a hangover is some kid yelling at a snail. Once She had her coffee and I had some ice water, we went outside. There were three of them down on all fours right in our yard; they explained it all to us. Their version of the story was that they were answering an urgent appeal from the zoo for snails to feed a pregnant hornbill. She said that was all very well and good but couldn't they catch the things quietly? If She were a snail, She said, she would have been several miles away by now after all that noise. The Boy Scouts looked at her as if She were the kind of person who would starve a hornbill mother, while I, of course, was wondering about the snail's viewpoint.

I found out after She had gone to work. I was in the backyard when I saw the merest trace of a movement in the grass. There was the most scared looking snail you ever saw, cowering under a rose bush. I said it could relax, they had gone, and the snail said it hadn't relaxed in days, not since this massacre began. I said I hadn't heard about it, and the snail said, well, hornbills didn't eat golden retrievers, and that was probably why, but if I were a snail, I would have heard about it.

I asked why they needed so many snails, and the snail said that if the truth were told, they didn't, it was Boy Scout overkill. Hornbills, it explained, were partial to snails, and the zoo was very proud of its hornbills, which are rare Southeast Asian birds that the snail said he personally thought were rather ugly. They dined most of the time on fruits and vegetables and a little dog food, he continued, but when a hornbill was pregnant, what she really liked for dinner was snails. I said, not too tactfully, that a lot of people liked snails, too, and he said I didn't have to remind him of that, he had lost eighty-nine members of his family to a recent dinner in a fancy French restaurant. In any case, what happened was that the zoo put out a request for people to bring in snails for the hornbill and the Boy Scouts had taken it up as a cause and were hounding every snail for miles around.

He said he hadn't slept in days and might never sleep again if that damned bird didn't hurry up and hatch her egg. I told him I sympathized, and he said I ought to, especially considering what a horrid death it was. Did I know, asked the snail, what was involved in a snail dinner in a hornbill household? The husband hornbill crunched up the shell, chewed up the snail, and tossed the whole thing to his greedy spouse. I said uneasily, not having had any breakfast at that point, that I hadn't known, and I wished I had never found out. The snail nodded bleakly, and said it had better be moving on before those young monsters came back. I asked if I could give it a ride somewhere safe, and it said, how about Peru?

When I thought about it later, it did seem hard on the snail. Sort of like a snail pogrom, I suggested to Joseph, who had crept by on what he likes to call his morning constitutional. There you go again, said Joseph, happy for the excuse to stop moving, seeing sociological implications burgeoning all around you. I said he might be less blasé about it if he were a snail, and Joseph said that if he were a snail he would have had the sense not to hang around discussing the digestive habits of hornbills when there was a pack of Boy Scout vigilantes on his trail. He had some feeling for their situation, he said, but he had heard, as the snail apparently had not, the zoo's second SOS, which was for God's sake to take it easy on the snails. The energetic Scouts, he said, apparently had been bringing in bucketsful of snails every time it rained, which was frequently at that time of year. The hornbills couldn't consume them all, and the excess had been dumped in the zoo gardens, much to the dismay of the gardeners, who found that the snails were gobbling up the zoo's pet plants.

You see, said Joseph, there's a natural course of events that neither you nor this snail even considered. If he and his kind had hidden until the uproar was over instead of taking undue risks in backyards full of Boy Scouts, far more of the species would have survived. Come to think of it, he said, didn't your owner have snails for dinner the other night? I looked around uneasily. I thought so, said Joseph, and didn't you tell me she offered you one and that you—I asked him please to keep his voice down and peered nervously at the grass under my feet. Joseph, who has a mischievous streak, waited—deliberately I'm sure—until he saw a snail before asking me what escargot tasted like.

# Chapter 16

I have never been psychoanalyzed, nor do I feel any need for it, so I was astounded the other day when Joseph announced that his owners had taken him to a pet psychiatrist. I asked why, and Joseph said they thought he was depressed. Was he depressed? I asked. Not especially, said Joseph, it was just that he meditated a lot, and most people couldn't tell the difference in dogs. I asked what it was like, and Joseph, who is of a patient and tolerant nature, said it was quite interesting although not very useful. It was his opinion, he said, that only people could trust psychiatrists; dogs had too much common sense to pay much heed to a man who apparently couldn't tell a dog from a whale.

How was that? I asked. Joseph said, well, this man, who seemed perfectly amiable in other respects, seemed to feel that dogs were being given too much equality. The way he put it, it was all right to claim equal rights for whales, who were in the middle of an ocean, but it was quite another thing to give equal rights to a dog in the middle of the living room. The logic of this, said

Joseph, as far as he could tell, appeared to be that a whale wasn't going to bite people in the middle of the ocean. I said that in my view equality for dogs had not even been glimpsed. Joseph said he knew my liberal politics would have led me to that conclusion, but he found the psychiatrist's remark more significant in that it indicated people were still basically afraid of animals.

Ridiculous, I said. How could anybody in his or her right mind be afraid of someone like Joseph? He nodded, and said that, of course, was true, he was probably the most polite and least intimidating of dogs, yet he still belonged to another species, one that people believed they had tamed and controlled. I admitted that in comparison with what were called wild animals we probably were controlled, and Joseph said, well, wild animals were our equivalent of criminals at large, although he personally thought even wild animals behaved with more dignity than most criminals. I thought about it and said he had an excellent point. Joseph, who had been studying a cluster of daisies, said he was glad I agreed with him, not that it would have changed his mind if I hadn't. I asked what else the psychiatrist had said, and Joseph said he had reassured his owners that Joseph was not depressed, only a little bored.

How had he known that? I asked. He hadn't, said Joseph, but on the other hand, his owners were paying this man for these opinions and presumably he had to tell them something. The problem was, said Joseph, that he was a remarkably well-adjusted dog, who gave the psychiatrist no trouble at all, and he suspected that a few well-defined neuroses would have made the man's task much easier. Basically, the psychiatrist thought the trouble with animals nowadays was that people treated them too much like people and it confused them. The people? I asked. The animals, said Joseph.

Why would it confuse them? I asked. Well, said Joseph, yawning, it was the psychiatric theory that a dog was a dog was a dog, so to speak, and if you treated it like your father or your sister or your husband, it forgot what it was supposed to be and started acting like what it was being treated as. I said I understood neither the theory nor his syntax, and Joseph said I had asked and he was trying to tell me and, if I was going to be difficult, he would simply take his morning nap, which was long overdue. What he thought it meant, he said, was that dogs who were treated like people become overprotective of those people and bit other people, which could lead to problems for that dog with other people. Was that clearer? Not much, I said, but I got the idea, and it still made very little sense. For example, I said, I was quite protective of my owner because it seemed to me She needed some protection, but only up to a certain point. I was aware of what I could and could not do and I had no desire to be her husband, whatever that was supposed to mean.

Joseph said he never supposed I had any problems along those lines; if anything, he had always thought I was too much of a dog. I said I was not prepared to argue with him and what were they going to do about his alleged boredom? Joseph said as far as he could tell, they were going to talk about it at infinite length to dinner guests, none of whom had ever taken their dog to a psychiatrist, and they would dine out on the whole episode for years. So it seemed that everyone had benefited, said Joseph. The psychiatrist had earned himself some money, his owners had become social curiosities, and he had behaved so well with the doctor that he had been rewarded with a filet mignon. Then he went to sleep.

# Chapter 17

Sometimes I think there is no limit to the lengths to which people will go. We were all reading the papers together this morning, more or less. She throws the papers on the floor, which annoys both Charlie and me, because we are more tidy-minded than She is, and we like our papers in order. He casts an exasperated look at me as we paw through the pages. She doesn't so much read a newspaper as splash her way through it, and of course Charlie has a well-organized legal mind. Not unlike mine, I suspect. She and I have read the papers together for years and She always made a big joke out of my reading the funnies, saying didn't I just love Snoopy and Fred Basset. I notice Charlie doesn't do that. In fact, I noticed Charlie watching me with a rather peculiar expression the other day as I was scanning the new Reagan foreign-policy speech. It's not that I dislike the funnies, although Snoopy does seem to me a little too unkind to Charlie Brown—I could never treat *her* like that. I lean toward Fred Basset, who is more the philosophical type.

But, to return to the latest atrocity, there was this

lengthy article in the paper about a veterinarian who recommended puncturing your pet. I could hardly believe the headline and I didn't blame Charlie for uttering an astonished guffaw at the idea. He and I are turning out to have remarkably similar reactions, which just goes to show you shouldn't make snap judgments about people. Anyway, this man actually advocated acupuncture for a dachshund with a slipped disc, or a horse with the heaves, or a senile cat. I noticed he said cats tended to be needle-shy, which is no more than I would expect of a cat; that species is well versed in self-preservation.

Horses and dogs were "most receptive," according to the article, which may tell you more about horses and dogs than I care to accept. Horses, said the vet, were "not the most intelligent of animals," but bright enough to know when they were receiving what he described as "positive energy." The only sensible thing he had to say was that people who wanted to try acupuncture on a horse should watch out while manipulating its hind legs. Apparently dogs just put up with being stuck full of needles, on what I consider the dubious theory that what feels good to an owner will feel good to a pet. I have had a touch of arthritis in my hip from time to time, but as far as I know, acupuncture has not even proved entirely effective even on humans. As far as I'm concerned, its just one more example of pets being put upon by people.

I was relieved to see the other day that a group called Attorneys for Animal Rights has been founded in California, as well as a new political-action committee called ROAR, or Respect Your Animals' Rights, and I hope they are paying attention to this acupuncture business. They do seem to have had some success in putting an end to that brutal practice of sawing off elks' antlers so they can be ground up and sold as an aphrodisiac. I have no idea whether powdered antlers actually do improve people's performance in the bedroom, but my sympathies are entirely with the elk in this case.

I was saying to Joseph the other day that it seems to me animals are the last minority. Cases of discrimination absolutely abound, and people seem to think it's funny. For example, poor Stanley the lion was devoiced because it upset the neighbors when he roared. Now he mews, which is a disgraceful thing for a lion, and the neighbors are worried that he might sneak up on them. Personally speaking, I hope he mews while he eats them.

And then there's Conrad, that sea lion over in Santa Barbara who bays at the moon. Sea lions have always bayed at the moon, and why not? They haven't clipped his vocal cords yet, but they're going to send him to a psychologist. What a psychologist can do for Conrad, I can't imagine. The firm that volunteered specializes in something called stress training, which is one of those phrases people seem to use when they don't really know what they mean. I don't have much faith in the theory that stress training will persuade Conrad to be quiet, and if they're going to have zoos, what do they expect anyway? The only intelligent politician I ever heard of suggested that animals should be freed and people put in cages.

As I recall, it was just after that unfortunate hippopotamus, Bubbles, ran away from Lion Country Safari and met an untimely end, and this candidate for governor, Lowell Darling I believe his name was, suggested it would solve the unemployment problem if they let the animals out of the zoos and replaced them with people dressed in animal suits. It would be easier on the animals, too.

She said I looked cross this morning, and Charlie said, with remarkable perception, that if I had been reading that ridiculous story about the elephant who had been taught to roller-skate, no wonder I looked that way. It was more likely disgust, he suggested, and looked pleased when I gave him a brief lick on the wrist.

# Chapter 18

Joseph was sounder asleep than usual when I went looking for him this morning, but I did run into a really interesting cockroach on the patio. Talking to him cheered me up. When you think what cockroaches have lived through and how well they have not only endured but overcome man's efforts at extermination, it gives you hope. Once you get a cockroach talking, it is fascinating, especially if you find one with a little historic knowledge. This fellow, who said his name was Thomas, was pretty pleased with himself and, if what he told me was true, he had good reason. Actually, I see no reason to doubt him. Some government outfit, it seems, has been trying to seduce cockroaches —a dirty trick, in my opinion. The gambit was apparently something like come into my parlor, said the spider to the fly, except this was a synthetic that was supposed to fool the cockroach into thinking that what lay ahead, so to speak, was another cockroach and not some poisonous glue.

Thomas said he and most of his friends had been

around long enough to know the difference between a sexy lady cockroach and a synthetic mix. He said he didn't know any of his breed who had made this particular mistake, and it would serve humans right if the glue turned out to be lethal to them and their pets. I said I begged his pardon, and he said, no offense, but it was a jungle out there.

I replied a little stiffly that I was sympathetic to his problems, but I certainly wasn't looking for any more of my own; it was bad enough making sure that She fed me hamburger instead of that glop they advertise in television commercials. Thomas said he was really sorry, it had been a slip of the tongue and there wasn't a dog or cat he would want to see suffer because of something a cockroach didn't think was fit to eat. I couldn't get quite as upset about cats, but it had occurred to me that Joseph, whose eyesight isn't what it used to be, not that it was ever great, is inclined to eat anything, including the blue wool sock his owners put on his leg once to protect a sore. He said later it hadn't tasted too bad, although it made his tongue furry, but it certainly hadn't been as peculiar as the magazine page they next wrapped around the bandage. That tasted a bit like charcoal, said Joseph, and it hadn't done anything except give him bad breath, which his owners complained about even more than they had complained about his chewing on his bandages. I explained this to Thomas, who said he could see why I would be worried; it sounded as if my cousin needed a chaperone, or was he just dumb?

I wasn't about to hear criticism of Joseph from an insect, so I said that eye problems were common to all species and that dogs who had not been persecuted the way cockroaches had were much less likely to go through life full of suspicion. Thomas said that might be true but this latest devilish device was bound to get everyone in trouble.

What device? I asked. Thomas asked hadn't I heard about the electromagnetic flying saucers that sent out an absolutely agonizing high-pitched sound. I muttered nervously that I hadn't and how did he know about them? Thomas said a friend of his who acted as a spy for the species in a local entomological laboratory had told him about it. The idea was that the ultra-high-frequency sound would make insects disoriented so that they would either stagger off and get themselves squished or subside into a trance so deep they would neither eat nor even want to screw. It was supposed to work on mice, rats, and gophers, too, he added.

What about dogs? I asked. He said it was being sold to the Environmental Protection Agency on the grounds that it was not supposed to affect domestic animals, whatever that meant. I knew as well as he what those frequency aberrations were like, said Thomas. I shivered and said yes, I did, and it was a grim prospect. However, said Thomas, who had apparently saved the good news for last, the things were going to be very expensive, from what his friend had heard at the lab, and most people wouldn't be able to afford them, so he expected that private houses would be safe.

I said that didn't cheer me up too much, and Thomas said with a swashbuckling air that cockroaches had survived everything else and he was sure they would live through this, too.

House animals, he said a little patronizingly, would simply have to learn from the insect world. I said I expected that was true, and they certainly were an example to us all, at least as far as survival went. Thomas bridled a bit and said the cockroach was an example of what was best in the non-human world. I restrained an impulse to step on his conceited little face as I left.

He was right about his species, however, and I suppose if you are a cockroach, you have to develop a positive self-image. I have often marveled at the speed with which a cockroach can disappear, achieving cover even before She has screamed and flung her shoe. She always expects *me* to do something about them. She seems to view me as a combination of General Patton and Captain Marvel—or should I say the Incredible Hulk? I don't really mind her having such a touching faith in me as her protector, but I usually manage to warn any wandering mice or bugs to get out of her way. I'm certainly not going to annihilate them for her. One has to look out for one's own, after all, even if it is an inferior breed.

And speaking of mice, She mentioned the other day that she was working on a story about a $2 billion power plant that might be delayed because it was likely to disturb the territory of the salt-marsh harvest mouse, a nice little beast with an orange belly whom I have run into occasionally and found to be most sociable.

For once, the scientists appear to be on our side, one of them even going so far as to describe the mouse as "fragile, beautiful, and placid," which, of course, is a lot more than you can say for most people. Or any cats. Anyway, the way She described it, if the power plant is going to mean the end of the marsh mouse, there will be no power plant. You can imagine the reaction of the utility companies, who are visualizing another snail darter on their hands. The whole thing really brightened my day. The more I think about it, the more I consider it a good omen, and perhaps I should wake up Joseph and tell him.

# Chapter 19

Sometimes Joseph is not very satisfactory company, but this time it was really my fault. I should have remembered how bad tempered he is when awakened from his nap. He said he didn't care about the marsh mouse, and asked if I had thought what the lack of that power plant would mean—more electrical shortages and brownouts and blackouts; refrigerators that didn't work, which would mean no ice cubes for my martinis. He had never known, he grumbled, any other member of our family who wandered around all day collecting these odd pieces of information when he could be more healthfully and peacefully asleep. He supposed it must be my owner's occupation that had contaminated me.

I am fond of Joseph, but I felt this was too much to take, just because I had aroused him from a nap. I suggested he might live to be grateful for my information-gathering, because some day it might save his life. Joseph yawned, and before he could go back to sleep, I told him about the high-frequency flying saucer device. He said cockroaches were notorious for exaggeration, as well as being subject to paranoia, and he for one did not intend to disturb himself about it. I said crossly that he was becoming quite self-centered in his old age, and Joseph said that was an interesting observation, since I was two weeks older than he. But he did not want me to think he was uninterested in my eccentric companions, he said in a tone I could only consider condescending. I said I was sure it would be of little interest to him what animals were suffering at the hands of people, but I mentioned the plight of Stanley and Conrad.

Joseph said he could sympathize with their neighbors. He recalled one time when his owners had taken him with them on a trip and they all stayed in a motel next door to a zoo. He had not had a wink of sleep because of all the squealing and yowling and roaring and barking. He certainly would not care to live in such a neighborhood, and if they should ever choose to move to one, he might have to bestow his presence on another family, even though, he added, he knew it would break his owners' hearts.

That was what I meant, I said. Totally self-centered. Who wasn't? asked Joseph in a bored voice. As far as he could tell, it was the only way to lead a comfortable life, with all the small luxuries and attentions one required. Was I any less self-centered because I spent my days fuming over the inadequacies of people or complaining about my owner's male friends? Although, he mentioned, he had noticed I hadn't said a word in days about this Charlie person, so he assumed I had browbeaten him into serving me martinis and allowing me to demolish my liver the way I preferred it to be demolished. Joseph put his paws over his eyes in that exasperating way he has of indicating he's said all he has to say and wants to hear no more. Then, apparently sensing my resentment, he raised one paw and said why didn't I go and grumble to that ugly cat I was always gossiping with and see if I got any sympathy from him in my concern for animal welfare.

I was outraged and said so. Joseph muttered sleepily that he was sorry if he had upset me, but he had lately noticed I was becoming a hysteric and had developed a distressing habit of interrupting every little nap he ever took.

I said as far as I was concerned he could sleep until the following week without any interruption from me. Rhinestone Cowcat, I said bitingly, was better company, and perhaps more perceptive. Joseph's graying eyebrows rose to the tops of his ears and I took the opportunity to make what I considered a dignified exit. It would have worked, too, if his owners hadn't latched the gate so that I couldn't get out without nudging the catch around with my nose, which takes time and makes you look as if you are chewing on the lock. By the time I undid it, Joseph was snoring, although I was sure he was not asleep.

# Chapter 20

She is gone again, off to attend a rally of anti-nuclear demonstrators who are trying to stop the opening of a new atomic plant. She said it was an interesting story, but she was afraid that the demonstrators would be outnumbered by the reporters, who would all end up interviewing each other, as usual, and the biggest problem would be finding a parking space in the wilderness. I am certainly opposed to blowing up the world, although I expect people will manage to do it sooner or later. This, however, was one of those occasions when I was glad She didn't suggest I came along.

Once She took me to the Yosemite Valley where she was writing solemn stories about the National Park Service and where I found a much more intriguing story in the situation of some bears I ran into. Bears are pretty bored with people, by and large, but they have acquired a definite taste for certain junk food. One bear, who said his name was Jones, admitted that he had become addicted to waffles, and had come close to decapitating a backpacker who was unwilling to turn over his breakfast. It was difficult, said Jones, to go back to eating insects, berries, and the odd porcupine once you got used to gulping down Twinkies and pancakes slathered with syrup.

I mentioned that junk food wasn't good for him and the bear said didn't he know it, he had gained fifty pounds in six weeks and had been outrun by a tourist. It was humiliating. His father would have been horrified, he went on, to know that his son had developed an uncontrollable passion for waffles, and not even homemade waffles at that. It was the syrup at first, said Jones, and then he just became fond of the whole sticky doughy mess. He had once eaten seventeen waffles at a clip. That was the time he ran into a Boy Scout troop having breakfast and they ran away from him. It was a great morning, he added sighing nostalgically. I asked if his fellow bears were also hooked on human food and he said only some of them. It was partly the sugar, of course, said Jones, but a lot of bears were just concentrating more on the juicier redwood trees, which, he understood, was upsetting the rangers.

He wasn't as bad as some bears, Jones said in self-justification. He had friends who had actually learned to unscrew jar caps and demolish car locks just to get at the picnic baskets tourists had stored. They were especially fond of those packaged cream-filled cupcakes. The park service, he noted, was working at what he had heard them call bear-proofing in picnic areas, but all that did, said Jones, was to offer more of a challenge. It was a lot more fun for a bear to figure out how to take something apart the way it was supposed to be taken apart, scientifically, that is, instead of just using force. Any fool bear could rip something apart, he pointed out, but that way you might damage the food.

Or the people, I suggested. Jones shook his massive head. People weren't especially tasty, he said, and they were much too noisy. It was easier to get rid of them simply by charging. Very few tourists realized that when a bear really meant business, his ears were laid back when he charged. Of course, Jones acknowledged, not too many people had the self-possession to notice whether a charging bear had his ears laid back. The rangers knew about things like that, but they also had more sense than to go around gobbling waffles where a bear could smell them. He sighed. With the kind of diet he had become accustomed to, he said sadly, he might as well be in a zoo. His forebears would have been downright ashamed of him. It was too bad, I agreed, and it certainly wasn't good for him. Jones tossed me a quizzical look and suggested that I must have some bad habits, too.

Recalling that She and I had stopped for a snack at a picnic area on the way up and shared a shaker of martinis, I said nervously that I didn't know what he was talking about. Come on, said Jones, your breath could fell a redwood, and you're lecturing me about waffles? The conversation rather dragged after that and I left Jones looking hopefully at a newly erected tent. Back at the car, She was telling a ranger how worried She was about me. The ranger said that if I met a bear, I'd probably know what to do better than She would.

I suppose Jones made me think about the problems of co-existence between animals and people. Maybe the only way to escape corruption is to return to the wild, but that would have its disadvantages, too.

For one thing, I obviously have more in common with Jones than I care to admit, but I would have considerable difficulty adjusting to the outdoor life.

Just the thought of it makes my arthritis act up. It is a sad fact that those animals who have never crossed the threshold of the human world tend to view with contempt those of us who have become fellow travelers, as they used to say. For example, I have never met a coyote I could really like, and what's worse, I have never met a coyote who liked me.

Even Terminal Hate, who considers himself an outlaw, continues to eat Meow Mix in enormous quantities, not to mention the lion's share of any fresh fish his owners catch. Terminal Hate makes the best of both worlds, and I guess I have to admire him for that.

# Chapter 21

A whole slew of presidential candidates are announcing this week, so I'm alone again. And there's very little left in the Tanqueray bottle, which I hope Charlie will notice when he drops by to see me, as he said he would do while she's gone. I have to confess, a little to my own surprise, that I'll look forward to his visits. Not only do I miss her, but I've got accustomed to Charlie, and he continues to take good care of her, which takes a load off my mind and lets me worry about broader issues, as you might say. Joseph said I might not say it in front of him, because it was the most pompous thing he had ever heard and who did I think I was, Albert Schweitzer? Joseph is increasingly waspish these days. I think my remark about preferring to talk to Rhinestone Cowcat still rankles.

Today I decided it might cheer me up to go to the zoo, although once I got there, I felt I was turning into some kind of zoological social worker. Animals who live in cages seem to feel that because you don't, it is your duty to listen to their problems. This time I met Bouba and Abe, and as gorillas go, they were an interesting couple, especially since they were in the process of getting a divorce. I found out about that because Abe was sitting—cowering really—as far away from Bouba as he could get. I asked how things were going, and he told me in detail. It had been an awful two years, he said, since they brought him in to be Bouba's lover. Life with Bouba was like living with a female King Kong, said Abe, showing me his bruises.

I asked why Bouba was so difficult to get along with, and he said, well, she was a good deal older than he, to start with, and she was absolutely the bossiest gorilla he had ever met in his life. She had made life miserable for Albert, his predecessor, and when Abe arrived, the first thing she did was to slap him with a banana leaf. It was not, said Abe, the warmest welcome he had ever received, and eventually he had the feeling that even the keepers were jeering at him. It got so bad he was afraid to go into the sleeping enclosure where Bouba was waiting to pounce. Pounce how? I inquired. Not that way, unfortunately, said Abe. Bouba's pounce was anyone else's assault and battery. Why hadn't he defended himself? I asked. Bouba gestured toward the rear of the enclosure and I could feel myself backing off a little as I encountered the hostile stare of a gorilla who seemed to be about twice Abe's size. He had about as much chance of winning a fight with Bouba as I did, he said.

So he was leaving? I asked. Abe said, yes, he was going to a zoo in Texas where he understood that a female gorilla called Vanilla was awaiting him, or at least he hoped she was awaiting him, although he didn't think anything could be worse than what he had lived through with Bouba. I asked what was going to happen to Bouba, and Abe said he had heard the keepers say she was being moved to Pennsylvania where some unfortunate new mate called Henry was being prepared for her.

Maybe Bouba didn't want a lover, I mused.

Abe said there was no way she could know until she tried it. You mean she hasn't? I asked. Exactly, he said, at least, not with him, and he had heard that poor old Albert had fared even worse. Henry, he said, had his sympathy. She was also ugly, he added, ducking as a rock flew past his head, just missing mine. I excused myself before Bouba lost her temper and made my way home, pausing beside a tree only to see Terminal Hate's malevolent orange face in its branches. He said he had been stalking a gay gull, and snickered when I looked startled. One of that colony from the Santa Barbara Islands, he said. It had flown inland because it was lonely, or that was what it had been telling Joseph when he happened upon the scene. Where was the seagull now? I asked nervously. Terminal Hate sighed, and said it was fast off its mark. He had been going to prove to it that he harbored no discriminatory feelings at all about deviant birds. I said I didn't think that was a kind way to put it and Terminal Hate replied that it was because of soppy liberals like me that all these nuts were running around the streets and had I heard about that dumb friend of mine?

Cautiously, I asked which dumb friend, and he said, Dickens, of course. Was he lost again? I asked resignedly. Terminal Hate said, no, this time he had eaten nine brass padlocks. Nine? I asked. Terminal Hate sharpened the claws on his left paw and said they hadn't known about the other eight until the vet opened him up. They had been padlocking the chain that attached him to his kennel, and every time the padlock was unlocked, Dickens had chewed on it. When he got tired of chewing on it, said Terminal Hate, he swallowed it.

I said I supposed there was a certain logic to that, especially as far as Dickens was concerned. Terminal Hate said as far as he knew, Dickens did not subscribe to logic of any kind and maybe that made a certain kind of good sense. He looked at me closely and asked why I looked so down in the mouth. Frankly I was surprised he noticed. I told him about Abe and Bouba and Terminal Hate snorted, as I would have expected. He had no sympathy for a gorilla who couldn't handle a feisty female. Abe was a disgrace to gorilladom, said Terminal Hate, stropping the claws on his right paw with more than usual ferocity. I said I had seen Bouba and she was a formidable figure. That was because no one had ever taught her her place, said Terminal Hate, with an air of having solved the whole problem.

# Chapter 22

She is still away, but I feel quite cheerful. One reason is that I had a most interesting meeting with a unicorn. The other is that Charlie has been good company. He stops by in the evening, which is when I get most lonely, and we share a drink together. He is always careful now to pour mine into one of those nice crystal bowls; I still don't think he believes I really know the difference, but She once told him I was a terrible snob about what I ate out of. It's true I dislike plastic, but I don't mind pottery, as long as it's clean. Anyway, he pours and we sit in a companionable silence or sometimes he talks to her on the phone. Although he knows better than to do something idiotic like saying, Joe wants to talk to you, he sometimes puts the receiver down where I can hear her voice, and that's rather pleasant. Terminal Hate says he is just buttering me up, and perhaps he's right. But I might like him anyway. I don't like him the way I like her, and if they broke up I would still be prepared to bite him. But otherwise we seem to rub along increasingly well together.

To get back to the unicorn, however. I had read a good deal about him, and I had my doubts, but I went over to Marine World and there was Lancelot, already suffering from the problems that accompany fame. I must admit I found him convincing, and, in any case, how can anybody prove he isn't a unicorn? I mean, how many people have seen one? It was quiet when I ambled by the little castle where Lancelot lives in the Gentle Jungle section, and he was most hospitable, although his keeper was a little nervous about me at first.

Lancelot said he was delighted to see someone who wanted to talk about something besides whether or not he was real. I assured him I had never doubted it, and Lancelot said, well, it was kind of me to say so, but he doubted I had never doubted it, because there were times when even he wasn't too sure who or what he was. How was that? I asked. Lancelot said, well, he was sort of a concoction of a creature, bred by a couple up in Mendocino County who had announced he was the real-life version of a four-thousand-year-old secret. And wasn't he? I asked.

Lancelot said he suspected he was a bit of a mix who had turned out well. Not, he added hastily, that he doubted he was a unicorn. His original owners had been quite emphatic about that, and he supposed they knew what they were doing. What were they doing, actually? I asked. Lancelot said he had heard they were really into dragons, and were sort of practicing, when they came up with him. I admired the horn in the middle of his forehead and his cloven hooves, and he said if the horn went on growing at the rate it had been doing, they would have to expand his house. I said I expected there was a cut-off point, so to speak, and Lancelot said he certainly hoped so. He had been sharpening it, on the theory that doing so would discourage growth and the other day he had almost disemboweled a small boy who had rushed at him unexpectedly.

Perhaps, I suggested, they should pad the end of it, but Lancelot said it just wouldn't look right to have a unicorn running around with a cork on his horn.

I said I supposed he was right, and asked whether being a unicorn had endowed him with any insights from previous lives. Lancelot said he was still pretty new in this life, and was trying to hang onto the identity he had, although it wasn't easy, with all those scientists running around denouncing him as a fake.

I said I thought that was unfair and he said what had hurt most was the animal specialist who had called him a congenital anomaly, which made him sound as if he were retarded. It had not made him feel any better, said Lancelot, when the same man expanded the insult by explaining that the so-called "unicorn" was nothing more than an angora goat with a growth on its face. They could say what they liked, said Lancelot indignantly, but what he had growing on his forehead was a horn, and he ought to know, after all.

I advised him to ignore such slanders. Scientists were not generally popular even with people, as they were harbingers of bad tidings and stubbornly skeptical about what was obvious to everyone else. A scientist, I told him, was never happy unless he was the one to discover you or invent you, and if he hadn't, then you didn't and couldn't exist. No doubt, I said, that was why they were always quarreling among themselves. They could never accept the worth of anyone else's work and, of course, anything not subject to scientific proof they simply dismissed as apocryphal. Somebody had actually called him that, Lancelot admitted gloomily. Blazing new trails was always difficult, I told him encouragingly, and I bet the children believe you're a real unicorn.

Lancelot brightened and pawed the ground with one of his cloven hooves. That was certainly true, he said, and seeing them gaze at his horn was always the high point of his day. Although one child, obviously of scientific bent, had tried to pull it off and had to be physically discouraged by a keeper. He could have put a dent in the kid with his horn, said Lancelot, but he didn't want to damage his public image, especially as he had heard they were planning a movie around him.

I said he ought to be careful not to become too commercialized or he might end up on television lapping up unicorn munchies. As a matter of fact, I mentioned, I had recently run into a burro who had become so corrupted that he was addicted to junk food. Lancelot tossed his horn a little and said, well, what he had in mind was not watching, but participation. He might enjoy being on the Johnny Carson show, for example, he said. How did he know so much about television anyway? I asked. Lancelot looked a little sheepish and said his keeper watched it at night and he watched with her. Come to think of it, he admitted, he had developed a bit of a taste for potato chips. I didn't happen to have any with me, did I? I said I didn't eat junk food, and thrust out of my mind the image of Terminal Hate sneering at my own bad habits.

Lancelot looked so chastened that I apologized for not having any potato chips. He said meekly that if I didn't think he should eat them, I was probably right. There were a lot of things he was still learning. I said I thought he was fine the way he was and how could he do any better than to be a mythical beast in an age when nobody believed in anything? Lancelot said that was the nicest thing anybody had ever said to him, and he would swear off junk food. I said that was terrific and I was sure my friend the burro would never show that kind of self-discipline. Lancelot nodded complacently and then said, well, he might have to eat some of it as part of his television career but he would keep in mind my advice.

# Chapter 23

I had a visit from Joseph this morning, which was unusual since it was early and he seemed downright alert. In fact, he looked almost mischievous, which made me wonder if his owners had been giving him those megavitamins again. The last time they did it, he developed insomnia and they spent a miserable two weeks until he got the vitamins out of his system. He kept scuffling around the house at night bumping into things and wheezing until his owners had to buy themselves some tranquilizers. Joseph said it served them right; taking naps did not signify ill health but merely a normal desire for rest and quiet. He was more than usually lively this morning, however, and I just wondered.

He came strolling in and said he wanted me to meet someone. I must have looked surprised because he chuckled and said that for weeks he had been listening to me grumble about what people did to members of our world, and now he wanted to introduce me to somebody who was avenging our kind. At that moment a large black bird flapped over the wall, perched on a patio chair, and appeared to throw up. I said what did it think it was doing and Joseph said he had invited it over. The bird, having disgorged its breakfast, said, hey there, its name was Harold and it was a black-crowned night heron. Better known as a squawk, said Joseph with an uncharacteristic snicker.

I said I had never heard of squawks and not much of black-crowned night herons and asked if it had some problem with its digestion. Harold belched and said, hell no, it was just that his folks were messy eaters, which was what was upsetting everybody in his hometown. Nearby? I asked nervously. Not too far, said Harold, and they were moving into new territory all the time. He spat something out of his beak, narrowly missing my paw, and out of the corner of my eye I saw Joseph smile. Maybe he should explain, said Harold, why his people were so unpopular with humans. Maybe he should, I said, gritting my teeth, as I imagined what She would say about the mess on the patio. Harold fluffed his feathers and scattered droppings on the chair where he perched. Once, he said, squawks were almost extinct, which had made them an endangered species. They were still protected, he added hastily. He was a protected species? I asked bleakly. Harold nodded, scratching vigorously beneath his left wing.

Nobody, he said, had been allowed to touch a black-crowned night heron for years, and as a result they had undergone quite a population explosion, to the point where they were taking over small towns. Squawks, as they were locally known—at least that was the only name he thought he had better repeat in polite company, said Harold with a hoarse chuckle—liked to perch in trees, and that was where they liked to eat. I was beginning to see the extent of the problem. You mean you drop bits of food on the ground? I asked. Not on the ground, said Harold, usually on the people, because these are big old trees we sit in, and food isn't all we drop, heh, heh.

I shuddered, and avoided looking at Joseph. Not only that, continued Harold, but squawks were night birds. After a good day's sleep, they liked to be up and about, raising hell all night. I asked if they had loud voices, which was a mistake. Harold opened his beak and the piercing sound that came out was an ear-shattering cross between a quack, a screech, and a yowl. It was quite clear to me why they were known as squawks. What made it all so funny, said Harold, was that there was nothing that could be done to get rid of him and his thousands of friends and relatives. Nothing? I asked. Not a damned thing, Harold chortled, because, as was usual with people, while they all wanted to do something about the squawks, nobody could agree on what to do about them. Once, he related, the fire department had been called in to wash the squawks out of the trees, and the local bird lovers had risen up in outrage. Then the police had arrived, their guns loaded with blanks called bird bombs that were meant to scare the squawks out of the trees. It didn't bother the squawks, but every pet owner in town began calling in to complain that their dogs were having hysterics.

I said I did not think dogs had hysterics, but it was true that harsh sounds could upset them. Well, said Harold, it might have been the owners who were having hysterics, but the police force, all four of them, damn near got lynched. I asked what the current situation was and Harold cawed raucously. The way it looked now, he said, the people might move out before the squawks did, then things would be the way they were before the humans arrived, which might be an improvement. Meanwhile, he thought the whole thing was just hilarious.

I said it certainly had its ironic side, didn't it? Harold uttered another of those hideous sounds and flapped off, distributing a fallout of food scraps as he went. I looked gloomily at the evidence of his presence, which was even worse than I had thought. Then I looked at Joseph and asked if he thought all this was funny. Joseph said he thought it was quite remarkably funny and if I could stop being such a Pollyanna, so would I. The squawks, he pointed out, were flapping, filthy proof that the world of birds and animals would survive the world of people, and wasn't that what I kept brooding about? He said he didn't understand me; I got all worked up about man's injustice to other species and then, when man turned around and let a species get away with murder, I turned my nose up at it. So the squawks weren't too dainty, said Joseph. They were winning, weren't they? And wasn't that what I wanted? I said that his was a thoroughly simplistic attitude toward the problem of living in harmony, and Joseph said, for God's sake, didn't I even think this was funny? I thought for a moment and visualized that small town full of squawks and despite myself I chortled. Joseph said he wanted to make sure I wasn't becoming a misanthrope just because She had forgotten to replenish the gin before She left. I asked how he knew and he said I had been wearing the expression of a dog deprived for days.

# Chapter 24

She came back last night full of political chatter, and among the first things she did was buy a half gallon of Tanqueray gin and hug me several times. Charlie was working late, or She might have hugged him first, but I try not to think about that kind of thing, especially since he was very decent while she was gone. I lapped a little gin while she went through her mail, reading me bits and pieces out of her letters, a habit it took Charlie a while to get used to, but which I enjoy. Then she announced we were going for a walk, which surprised me. She usually just tells me to take a walk and not get lost, which I did once or twice when I was younger. I must have looked surprised, because She laughed and said I had raised my eyebrows and maybe we should just talk about it over a drink, so I arranged myself more comfortably on the rug beside the sofa and She poured another drink and said She had been thinking about me while she was traveling and thought I didn't get enough exercise. She and Charlie had been talking about taking up jogging, She said, and how would I feel about that?

*Chapter 24*

I growled. Softly, but I growled. I don't mind a good brisk walk, or even a run, but I have no desire to emulate those grim-faced people who go thudding sweatily by as I lie on the grass smelling the roses. She laughed even harder and said, well, she guessed she knew how I felt about that idea, didn't she? I looked at her anxiously and she hugged me (I suspect She had had a couple of drinks on the campaign plane before She got home) and said, well, maybe She would just let Charlie jog by himself, how about that? I licked her on the nose, which is unusually demonstrative for me. What we needed, She said untruthfully, was some more gin.

And She bounced up, opened the refrigerator and let out a shriek that must have done Terminal Hate's heart good. I knew immediately what was the matter, of course. Wilbur and Christopher were back.

I knew they were back because I had brought them back. I decided after I had cleaned up the mess Harold left—or at least, kicked it into one of her lilac bushes—that I ought to go check out those poor little mice. She prided herself on being an investigative reporter, and I took the position that Wilbur and Christopher were worth a little investigation in my world, even though laboratories make me almost as uncomfortable as a vet's office or a dog show. She took me to a dog show once; as a matter of fact, She entered me in my class as a fine upstanding representative of my breed and I have never been so embarrassed in my life. The whole thing made me feel as if I had been stuffed, and I was not about to put up with those tweedy, lumpy persons poking at my hindquarters. Or my front quarters, for that matter.

I did what any self-respecting dog would do. I bit the judge. Not hard, mind you, just a warning nip on the ankle and I'm sure it hardly broke the skin, although from the uproar he made, you would have thought I had gone for his throat. She ran around apologizing until She realized it was She I was glaring at. Although I would never bite her, I would ignore her around the house. I did that once and She was miserable because She isn't accustomed to my not fussing over her, but on that occasion, She had announced she was putting me on her vegetarian diet and I had to take a stand. Of course we got thrown out of the dog show and She said I had disgraced her. But She admitted the judge was a jerk so I think She was secretly rather proud of me.

Anyway, to get back to the mice. After Joseph said they had left the refrigerator to go back to the laboratory, I couldn't get the poor little things out of my mind, so I snooped around a bit with some other mice and a rat or two of my acquaintance and sure enough, they hadn't gone far. Not any farther than the swimming-pool shrubbery, to be exact. Christopher said it seemed warmer over there, as long as they stayed out of the draft. Wilbur was bothered by drafts. I asked why they hadn't gone back to the laboratory and Christopher said he was the one who had been reluctant. Wilbur was pretty comfortable there because he was a rare mutant and cherished, but this business of suspended animation and sleeping in freezers was worrying him. Christopher said he had a feeling some day he would freeze to death and he wanted to die somewhere warm.

Why couldn't he stay here and let Wilbur go back? I asked. Mostly, he said, because Wilbur couldn't remember where the laboratory was. That was when I decided it was time I took a more aggressive role in my world. I told Christopher I would find the laboratory and take Wilbur back. It wasn't quite as adventuresome as it sounded because I didn't think Wilbur could have traveled very far, so I figured the building had to be reasonably close by and I could carry him there in my mouth, which was designed for transporting birds at one time in my breed's past and would be equally comfortable for a bald mouse. Meantime, I said, where would they like to be? Christopher said they had really been quite happy in my owner's refrigerator, especially since it was set on low (that's because I like gin chilled but not icy). Fine I said, and we all trotted back to the house where I opened the refrigerator door for them. It was shortly afterward that She came back, which of course distracted my attention from my investigative activities.

She acted as if She had discovered Dracula in the refrigerator, hopping around and wailing at me to do something. So I set up a great growling and wuffling, which always makes her think I am taking care of her, and as soon as She locked herself in the bathroom, which is her response to such crises, I scooped them both up and whisked them out the back door. Christopher said he would be fine in the shrubbery and perhaps I would be kind enough to let him know when She was gone again since he didn't want to abuse her hospitality by scaring the hell out of her every time She opened the refrigerator. I said that would be fine, and asked Wilbur if he had any idea at all where his laboratory was.

Wilbur said the nice sleep in the refrigerator seemed to have refreshed his mind, because he could distinctly remember a street sign. Seventeenth, he thought it was. A big green building with a white front door. I was relieved, because I knew at once where it was. I had once waited there in the car for her while she did an interview with a man who was experimenting on beagles. We were both so mad about the whole thing that we finished a whole shaker of martinis when we got home, and I took pride in the fact that She wrote a story about it—not as strong as I might have done, but adequate—that caused such a fuss the project was halted, although I don't know if it was halted soon enough for the beagles. Anyway, I knew where Wilbur's laboratory was. I hoped he was having better luck there than the beagles, but I was beginning to learn that you can't live anybody else's life for them, even a bald mouse. Christopher might have been right when he said that as mice went Wilbur was a lucky mutant. The odds were that Wilbur's keepers would be overjoyed to see him.

I tucked Wilbur carefully into my mouth and set off while She was still in the bathroom and, apart from the fact that I had to be careful about remembering not to swallow, unaccustomed as I was to having a mouse in my mouth, we arrived without mishap at the laboratory. I thought I'd have to simply leave him on the steps, but then I saw it was a swinging door, so I thought I'd better get him safely inside and put him somewhere conspicuous so they wouldn't think he was just any old mouse. In the foyer, there was a list of offices, one of them marked "Research" and I figured if that wasn't it, they would at least recognize him. God knew he looked different from any mouse I had ever seen.

I went to the door of the research office, peered around, and saw a couple of men in white coats, so I opened my mouth, and out Wilbur popped. In case they hadn't noticed, I gave a soft bark, and that got their attention. They caught a glimpse of me and then they saw Wilbur, who was sitting sedately in the middle of the floor, waiting to be noticed. One said, my God, it's Wilbur, and from the tone of his voice, I knew Wilbur was going to be treated like a prodigal son, so I headed on home. As I went out the front door, I heard one of the men saying, who the hell was that dog that came in with Wilbur? Did you see that dog? And I chuckled to myself all the way home, where She was waiting to congratulate me on being her big brave protector who must be ready for a little drinkie.

I didn't know about that kind of nonsense, although I made allowances for her condition, but I certainly was not going to refuse a nice dry martini. It did occur to me, however, that maybe it was just as well that Charlie had not opened that refrigerator door, because now that he knew me better, he might have concluded that the presence of mice there, especially a mouse that looked as peculiar as Wilbur, had nothing to do with her housekeeping but might have involved me. Charlie has been looking at me a lot with a puzzled expression.

# Chapter 25

I never thought I would be putting *this* on paper, but I am seriously thinking of leaving her, and if I do, She will have this as a legacy, once I get it out from under the refrigerator which, I discovered recently, is leaking. I think even Charlie was surprised at her because he didn't say much while it was going on, and with him, that seems to be a sign of disapproval. He did say he thought She might be overdoing it, but then She flew at him, accusing him of being callous toward a helpless animal, and that exasperated me immensely. She and I have never had a serious disagreement before, but this business about the rats may be the end of our happy home.

It began when she was assigned to a sociological study on the relationship between animals and people, a subject on which I am far more of an expert than any of those pompous psychologists she interviewed. I thought it would be just more of the usual nonsense, but She came home full of gloom and doom and when Charlie said what She needed was a drink, and I began wagging my tail, She started lecturing me on my habits. She had, She explained in a tone of voice one might use on a not-very-bright four year old, been told about this experiment in which rats were put in the rat equivalent of a condominium and trained to observe a cocktail hour. The results, She said, were that the rats went on a binge, got depressed, turned aggressive and developed hangovers in the course of which they slurped up huge quantities of water. My reaction was so what else was new? But She was just getting started, and I could hardly believe that She believed what She was saying.

Charlie, to give him credit, said, for God's sake, what did an experiment on rats have to do with Joe having a little nip now and again. She said she would thank him to keep out of what was between her and her dog and She only hoped She hadn't already ruined my life. What She was talking about, she explained grimly, was nothing short of corruption and degradation, and Charlie said, oh, come on, and She gave him a dirty look and went right on.

Normal rats, She said, did not behave like this, which meant that the condominoum rats were acting like people. I listened patiently to these obvious conclusions, assuming that at some point, She would pour me my evening martini. What She did was to pour herself her evening martini, while delivering a dissertation on the evils of alcohol that would have done justice to Carrie Nation. The evils of alcohol for animals, that is. People apparently were immune, the way She put it, or at least it was a conscious choice for them, a nice cop-out if ever I heard one. But they had NO RIGHT She said in her capital letters, save-the-sinner voice, to inflict this evil on helpless animals.

I sat and stared at her. I could not believe that this person, whom I had considered enlightened and perceptive could be mouthing this balderdash. Why would I drink something I didn't like, and who was She to think for me? I had done more research into the animal world—my world—than she would ever glimpse at her silly paper. When had a Med fly, a mouse, a gorilla, or a worm ever unburdened itself to her, and what a scoop it would be if one ever should! I was furious, and She didn't even seem to realize it. When She came over and put her arms around my neck and breathed the fumes of her second drink all over me and told me how sorry She was for what she had done to me and would I ever forgive her, I didn't even growl. I simply removed myself from her grasp and went through the kitchen door. If it had been closed, I would have gone through it anyway.

I heard her calling to me, and I could hear Charlie's voice making disapproving sounds at her, but I didn't stop. I marched straight over to Joseph's and for once he was not only awake, but attentive. Joseph does come through when you need him, I have to admit. He said I seemed to be distressed. I said that was an understatement and told him what had just transpired. Joseph shook his head and was sympathetic. It was not, he observed, that he especially approved of my liking for gin; indeed he had thought, once or twice, judging by my condition in the morning hours, that I had overdone it. But he agreed that my owner's rationalizations were deplorable. What were my plans? I said I wasn't sure and I didn't want to rush into anything silly.

Joseph suggested I try ignoring her and I said I had thought of that, but while it would upset her, it would not change her mind about my alleged depravity. I had seen her before, I said, when she was on a reform kick, and She became very emotional. Undoubtedly, said Joseph, my owner was on what was called a guilt trip about making an alcoholic out of her dog. I might recall, he said, his own experience with a canine psychiatrist, and he hoped She didn't think of that for me, since he doubted that my current frame of mind would result in anything less than a diagnosis of derangement. The trouble, he said, was the psychiatric theory that single women with male pets eventually treated them like husbands. That was patently absurd in the case of my owner, he admitted, but psychiatrists tended to cling to stereotypes, or they had in his own case. I shuddered. Joseph looked at me thoughtfully and said it might be salutary if I stayed out all night. He'd ask me to stay with his owners, but that would probably be the first place She'd look.

What I would like to do, I said, was go to the nearest bar. Joseph said he realized that, and before I did it, he wanted to point out that, in addition to confirming her fears, it undoubtedly would be the second place She'd look.

I thanked Joseph for his advice and plodded on down the street until I encountered Rhinestone Cowcat, Terminal Hate, and Dickens. It seemed an odd combination so I asked what they were up to. What did I think? asked Terminal Hate wearily. They were taking Dickens home, of course. I asked what had happened to his customary police escort and Rhinestone Cowcat said they had apparently changed the duty shift so that the current officers were new to the beat and not familiar with either Dickens' problem or his home address. Dickens said mildly that it was very kind of everybody but he was sure he could manage on his own. Terminal Hate said he didn't give a damn if Dickens never got home, but his owners always created such a fuss that the entire neighborhood joined in the search. The last two times it had happened, Terminal Hate went on, his owner had got drunk with Dickens' owners and he had never got any dinner. I said I might as well join them as I no longer seemed to have a home and Rhinestone Cowcat, who sometimes sounds a lot like her addlebrained owner, said, oh, goody, goody, another divorce in the neighborhood.

# Chapter 26

As if I weren't upset enough, I had to listen to Rhinestone Cowcat telling some sad story about how hard it was to catch rabbits now that people were eating so many of them because of the price of steak. Terminal Hate said he never had any trouble catching anything he wanted to catch, and he was sure his owner would serve him steak if he wanted it. Oh, said Rhinestone Cowcat, you're such a put-down artist, why can't you enjoy a social conversation like any normal animal instead of being so *macho* all the time. I could feel my eyebrows crawling up my forehead and wondered if there were some new pollution in the air that was bringing out madness. This was the first time I had heard Rhinestone Cowcat even talk back to Terminal Hate, let alone lecture him on his manners, which were close to non-existent anyway. Terminal Hate's eyes narrowed to mustard yellow slits, and he asked if she had been talking to that wimp with the white coat and crossed eyes who had just arrived in the neighborhood?

Rhinestone Cowcat twitched her tail coquettishly and said it was true that a *gentleman* cat had moved in three doors up and she did want to say there was a difference in the way he treated her, especially when she compared him to some she could mention. Treading on ever-thinner ice, she went on to say that when she thought of the perfectly delicious little plump mouse KandyKat had brought her the other day she wondered if Terminal Hate was losing his skill as a hunter. Why, she couldn't remember, for all his boasting, the last time——— At that point what I had been expecting happened. Terminal Hate swatted her across the nose, not hard by his standards but hard enough to evoke an earsplitting howl from Rhinestone Cowcat and a responsive cry from her owner, who apparently had been watching from a window. Terminal Hate groaned and suggested we all get out of there.

I nudged Dickens, who was in his usual happy haze, and we took off at a rapid pace while Rhinestone Cowcat's owner came pounding down the pathway, screaming imprecations at Terminal Hate, who spat at her as he left.

Assuming correctly that Rhinestone Cowcat's owner would make no real effort at pursuit, we slowed down when we got around a corner and I looked curiously at Terminal Hate. Given that he would resent any slurs on his ability to catch anything that moved, I said, he was more upset than I would have expected. Terminal Hate bristled. What the hell made me think she had upset him? he hissed. He had merely been reacting to her female stupidity. Had I seen that stupid big white cat who put on all sorts of airs and hardly ever left its yard? Rhinestone Cowcat was always mooning and tippytoeing around it. Disgusting, he called it. I called it jealousy, but I had too much respect for Terminal Hate's sharpness of fang and claw to say so at that moment.

*Chapter 26*

Dickens evidently had only just registered Rhinestone Cowcat's earlier remark about divorce, because he turned to me and asked what I meant about not having a home. Just what I said, I told him, and I recounted the story of the rats and my owner's sudden embrace of temperance for animals if not for people. Terminal Hate said that, as a matter of fact, he agreed with my owner about my drinking, but he would be damned before he'd let a human, especially a female, tell him how to run his life. He didn't drink himself, he said, but he was sure that if he wanted to his owner would go along with it. Owners, he said, in his favorite turn of phrase, had to learn their place.

Dickens, who was a dog of few words, probably because he had few thoughts, said he didn't think he would leave, if he were me. Why not? I asked. Why inconvenience yourself? he said. I had, he pointed out, a comfortable home that I had to myself most of the time and while I might sometimes be lonely, I'd probably appreciate my independence more if I had owners who dogged my every footstep and called the police every time I was half an hour late getting home.

I knew that Dickens' half hour was sometimes two days, but other than that, I could not disagree with him. Terminal Hate nodded and said that although he never thought he'd hear himself say it, Dickens had a point. Where else, he asked, would I find an owner so free with her gin? I pointed out that apparently She was no longer about to be so free with her gin and he seemed to have missed the point. Terminal Hate snarled that he wasn't going to be contradicted twice by two dingbats in one night, and what he meant was that She had always seemed like a pretty reasonable owner to him, for a human, and wasn't I jumping the gun, as usual? It seemed to him, he went on, elaborating, that it would have made a lot more sense to ignore the whole thing, act as if I didn't give a damn about drinking, and let it all blow over. This way, I had probably convinced her that her dog was a drunk. I looked at him sharply. Terminal Hate sniggered. Well? he asked. I swallowed what I wanted to say, and considered.

Perhaps I ought to give her another chance, I said. By now, she was probably frantic with grief over my absence. Terminal Hate said she had always seemed fairly sensible to him, but I might be right. I ignored him, and returned, prepared to be dignified but aloof, and to drink from my water bowl. When I got there, I found She had invited a bunch of her newspaper friends to join Charlie and her in a raucous post mortem over the political trip, and they had not only finished the Tanqueray but were well into the Gilbey's. She greeted me with a burst of laughter, which made my fur bristle. Here he is, my poor little drunken doggie, She shrilled.

I stalked past her on my way to the kitchen, evading sundry pats and scratches and rubs as I went. But as I passed the coffee table on which the drinks were set up, I took my revenge. I deliberately bumped against the table, a flimsy pedestal affair, and had the satisfaction of seeing their martinis in their laps and the shaker on the floor. She was furious. She leapt up and screamed that I had done it on purpose, and Charlie, who seemed more sober than the rest of them, said, come on, don't be an idiot. Of course he did it on purpose, said Charlie, thereby raising himself several degrees in my esteem. Any dog that's been put through what you put him through tonight would be entitled to show you what he thought of you. I walked back, stood before him, and wagged my tail. One of her drunken friends said I should be out in the yard where I belonged, she'd never seen such a spoiled animal, you'd think from the way they acted that I could understand what was going on.

She told her to get out, which was the least She could have done, of course, and they engaged in a nasty altercation about who was drunker. Meantime, Charlie and I went into the kitchen together and he offered me the remains of his drink. He figured I deserved it, he said. I drank it appreciatively, and as I was swallowing the last of it, She came bursting in and said what did he think he was doing to her dog? Charlie said Joe needed a man to understand him. She burst into tears, and Charlie and I finished the rest of the gin.

# Chapter 27

I left the house this morning before She was up, or I should say, before they were up. Charlie and She had a long talk after I made my decision to sleep in the back yard. I know it was a long talk because at the beginning I could hear most of it. Then her voice softened and so did his and I figured that maybe the worst was over. She came out and made overtures toward me, rubbing behind my ears the way She knows I like it, hiccuping a little, and saying She was sorry, She hadn't meant to hurt my feelings, She was just worried about me. I was touched by that, but I pretended to be asleep. I suspect I didn't fool her, but I knew She had Charlie, who I have pretty much decided is a decent example of a human, and I wanted to think, because I was considering what I believed to be a big decision. It occurred to me during the uproar last night that maybe I should leave my journal out where She could see it.

Perhaps it would be good for people to see themselves as we see them and, more important, to realize how much they underestimate what is around them. I went to sleep without making up my mind, and when I woke up, I strolled over to Joseph's house. He was lying down in a patch of sunlight, but he must have been waiting for me, because his eyes flew open in a most uncharacteristic manner and he sat up immediately and inquired how I was. I told him what had happened after I left him, and he nodded and said I had done the right thing, and that this person Charlie sounded as though he might be a good influence on my owner. I said that was a possibility, but it wasn't really what I wanted to talk about. Joseph noted that I seemed less obsessed on the subject of alcohol deprivation than I had been the night before, and I said I thought he might be right.

She and I probably did drink a bit too much at times, but what had really annoyed me was her sanctimonious attitude. Joseph said he could understand that; his owners were equally unreasonable about the number of naps he took. I explained to him about the journal I'd been keeping, and my thoughts about letting her see it. Joseph said he didn't know I could type, and I said I couldn't, or not very well, but it wasn't that difficult. Most people, I had noticed, used what they called a hunt-and-peck technique and that was what I had followed, with limited success. But I had managed to put things down, I said. Illustrations, too? asked Joseph. After a fashion, I said, there were illustrations, but more to convey a mood than to demonstrate artistic talent. Joseph nodded and said he thought it might be a worthwhile venture, assuming my owner had the intelligence to realize what it was. I said a little sharply that She was quite bright. My complaint had to do with her hypocrisy, not her intelligence. Joseph told me to simmer down. He was not insulting my owner, he said, although he probably could have done it with impunity the previous evening. He was trying to pay me a compliment and I was reacting in my usual prickly manner.

I apologized and said I was grateful for his comments and would be glad to let him read the manuscript. Joseph said, well, perhaps some time he would, but he had a feeling he had heard most of what was set down there and it would probably do more good for people to read it. My world, Joseph pointed out, was the world of Dickens and Terminal Hate and Rhinestone Cowcat and himself, not to mention that slew of strange characters I always seemed to be talking to, and it was their story I was telling as well as my own.

What he thought I should do, said Joseph, was to go home and rescue the manuscript before the leaks rendered it illegible, and leave it on the coffee table where She would find it. He hoped, however, that I realized what the future might hold. I said I didn't understand what he meant. Did he think She'd be angry? Heavens, no, said Joseph, who reminds me more and more of Eric Sevareid as he gets older and becomes more pontifical. She would undoubtedly rush to her newspaper with my journal in one hand and me in the other, proclaiming a world scoop, if that was what they still called it. I stared at him, and Joseph said impatiently that I couldn't be that dense. I had to realize the potential impact of the discovery that in between drinking martinis, a dog in a California suburb had been typing up what amounted to a critique of contemporary society and an unprecedented insight into the world of Med flies and mice and moths and bears and gorillas, all rolled into one. It was quite possible, said Joseph, that nobody had ever realized any of these species could think. I would probably end up on the talk shows and be ruined, he said, and went back to sleep.

I came home somewhat subdued. I drank some water, which probably *is* better for me, and fished my journal out from under the refrigerator. It was a bit damp and there were some mouse droppings on it, but it seemed to me to be legible. So now it is on the coffee table, and I am waiting for her to come home.

the end?

*Muriel Dobbin is a Scottish-born newspaper reporter now based in San Francisco as the West Coast bureau chief for the* Baltimore Sun. *Previously she spent several years covering the White House for the* Sun, *an occupation which may have contributed to her growing fondness for dogs. Unfortunately, she travels too much to own one herself, so she has made a best friend of Joe, a golden retriever who is, of course, a real dog. This is Joe's book, and a book for everyone who likes animals and believes their intelligence is underestimated, especially by politicians, of whom Ms. Dobbin has met quite a few.*